eVOICE

J. Price Blalock

To Lynn,

Always and all ways.

Contents

Chapter 1

The Package

"Did you see that?"

"Was it the signal?"

Two men were crouched out of sight, hiding in a recessed doorway at the corner of 1st and Main. The pair was draped in grey raincoats to protect themselves from the stinging wind-driven rain. It was three in the morning. The two stared across an empty street at one dull light illuminating the back stairs of an old two-story warehouse that had been converted into upscale condominiums. They had studied their plan over and over. They had talked about this night inside and out. The time to spring into action had finally arrived. Still, when the back door of the building cracked open and a thin red laser beam flashed out, the two men looked at each other in disbelief.

"About time, let's do this," Jack said in a raspy voice.

The second man, Tony, grunted his approval as he flipped his cigar back into the doorway and stepped into the howling rainstorm. Tony had wanted to carry his .38 revolver, but Pete, the signalman, was against it from the start.

"If someone catches you guys in there, it'd be my job and a quick deal with the court," Pete pleaded.

"If we carry guns and get caught, we're looking at some serious pen time, or maybe worse. You planning on dying over this?" Tony reluctantly agreed.

As Jack and Tony ran across the street toward the service entrance, Tony focused on the objective. This was the plan. No firearms. Fake a forced entry. Steal the rich guy's painting. Tie up the security guard, rough him up a little, then get the hell out. In and out, quick and easy. The whole heist wouldn't take ten minutes.

Pete was their inside man, the building's night security guard. The three spent days concocting a cover story for Pete, but once it was finalized they had faith it would be believed. After all, Pete was trusted by upper management and he had gained a little clout from working there for the past seven years. They deduced that no one, not even the cops, would suspect he was in on it.

Tony continued rehearsing the plan in his brain. It was simple, quick and easy. Make it look like Pete was blindsided, sell the painting, and split the dough. He was positive Pete would fool the cops. He was a professional liar and his other partner, Jack, knew how to cover their tracks.

Gordon Manners was the owner of this posh condo. And Pete, as the brain who originally hatched the scheme, was positive that Mr. Manners had come from old money. Through Pete's years of working as the glorified doorman, with his security station located in the swanky entrance of the converted warehouse, all three men were convinced Mr. Manners had plenty of the green stuff. So much green stuff that they felt a "redistribution of wealth" was in order.

Gordon didn't work the nine-to-five like they pounded out every day of their life. Gordon had fancy clothes, beautiful women, expensive cars, and plenty of good booze to wash it all down with. He slept until all hours of the day and partied every night. They figured him to be an old, rich, trust-fund baby. He wouldn't miss the painting.

"The painting's got to be insured anyways," Jack rationalized for them.

"Besides, this silver spooner only tipped me twenty bucks last Christmas. What an arrogant sonofabitch!" Pete would ramble to the other two often. It helped justify his guilt.

Tony and Jack made their way in through the back door as Pete held it open, the rain dripping from their raincoats into shallow pools on the wooden floor. After the two were safely inside, Pete scarred the door with a crowbar to make it look like a forced entry. The three men then bolted up the servant's stairway to Gordon Manners' condo on the second floor. Pete smiled and reached into his pocket for the key he had copied after Mr. Manners had stumbled drunk through the lobby late one night and dropped them. He returned the keys to Mr. Manners the next morning and no one was the wiser. The plan was in motion, luck was on his side. Easy enough.

"Cheap bastard didn't even tip me when I returned them," Pete cussed.

He had used the copied key to case the condo, which was how he first saw the painting, a Picasso. Millions of dollars just hanging on the wall of some rich yuppie's condo. The three figured they could at least get a quick 750k, maybe even a million, from a good fence. They had put the word out and met a gambler named Boxer, who was ready to pay cash for it upon delivery. Not a bad night's work, all things considered. Standing in front of the condo door, the three grinned as Pete pulled the key from his pocket.

Pete pushed the key into the tumbler, unlocking the door as he looked back at his partners with a sense of achievement. He pushed the door open and stepped into the condo. The sound was muffled, but the results were unmistakable. The hole that suddenly appeared in Pete's upper chest was huge. The impact propelled him back against the door jamb as he dropped to the floor in a loud crash. Jack and Tony felt the warm blood splash against their faces as they scrambled, helpless. More muffled shots then ripped from inside the condo into the door and plaster walls in front of them.

After the initial shots were fired, Jack didn't hesitate. He pulled a Colt 10mm from his raincoat and fired two shots as he stepped through the doorway. Both hit their target and the mysterious man firing from the middle of the living room crumpled to the ground.

"Jesus Christ! Pete!" Tony squealed as he kneeled down beside Pete, the blood spraying from his chest like a leaking garden hose.

Jack immediately moved across the room with military precision, the 10mm held at the ready. He swept the corners of the room first before he pointed the gun at the huddled man on the floor. Jack reached down and checked for vital signs. Two fingers against a still carotid artery.

"This guy's dead, too," Jack announced plainly, looking at two direct hits in the middle of the corpse's chest. He then reached down and put the dead man's gun under his raincoat.

"I thought we agreed we weren't gonna bring no guns," Tony's words trembled.

Jack coldly replied, "Tell that to Pete."

"Pete's dead, man! This is bad, man. This is bad, this is bad," Tony kept repeating those words as he stared at the lifeless body that was once his friend. Blood began to saturate Pete's shirt as it ran down the side of his neck and pooled onto the floor. Tony lost it and began to shake.

The Picasso they planned to steal was hanging on the wall. Its frame was supported by a long brass piano hinge that had been swung open like a cabinet door. Hidden behind the painting was safe. The safe was open.

"We gotta go, man! Screw that painting, Jack, we gotta bail," Tony stuttered as he stumbled out the door and ran toward the back staircase.

Jack remained calm. His eyes were fixed as he approached the open safe. It didn't take him long to survey the contents. Inside were two 8x10-inch manila envelopes, each about an inch thick. He grabbed the Picasso and jerked it as hard as he could, trying to rip it from the wall. It held firm. He heard a faint siren. There wasn't enough time to cut it out of the frame or unscrew it from the hinge, so he improvised, adapted. He grabbed the envelopes from inside the safe, shoved them into the back of his pants and followed Tony down the staircase and out into the black, wet night.

Chapter 2

Austintatious

It was not a depressing life. His parents had scoured old family names and agreed on Nathaniel Horace Level as their son's God-given one. He would have chosen a different name, but he wasn't given a vote at the time. His few friends called him Nate, everyone else just called him Mr. Level. His six-foot-three, two-hundred-and-ten-pound frame was in surprisingly good shape after enduring fifty-five years of fast living. As Nate pulled into his driveway and parked his new-off-the-line GMC Yukon 4X4 next to his wife's BMW, he downed the last swig of scotch he had poured for himself when he left the office. He preferred to park in the garage, but the eight-car garage was admittedly full. It housed the '65 baby blue Mustang convertible, the '59 red-and-white ragtop Corvette, two jet skis, a custom-built chopper, three ATVs, and a golf cart. It was suspiciously void of any shovels, rakes, lawn mowers, yard equipment, tools, or other clutter typically found in the average suburban garage. The "toy room," as he called it, was attached to an austintatious four-thousand-square-foot house built out of limestone and tinted glass. Littering the two-acre front yard were massive pecan and old oak trees. In the backyard, the volleyball pool, with a twenty-five-yard lap lane, opened onto a covered boat dock with two slips. It all attached to a pier that stretched a hundred feet out into the bay. Nate's newest toy, a twenty-six-foot rib inflatable, hung on a sling in the boathouse next to his Whaler.

"Why the hell do I have to go?" he whined under his breath as he walked through the medieval mahogany front door of his house.

"What did you say?" his wife, Sara, asked as she stepped from the bottom of a grand staircase onto the peach-colored marble floor in the foyer.

Sara was a petite woman. Five foot three with raven black hair that poured down to her shoulders. It stayed that color with the help of Clairol. She was two years Nate's junior and even after two children she managed to stay in great shape. Her slim figure was, in her own words, "under one twenty honey," which she would always say in a slow South Texas drawl. Sara had the face of a model, with high cheekbones, a chiseled nose, and sea green eyes. With the children grown and gone, she spent her days doing as she pleased.

Nate yelled across the foyer at her from the front door. "Gordon begged me to go to South America for him this time. I told him to forget it. They're your clients, you go!" he explained to her as he hung his suit jacket up on the teak hall tree.

"AAAAND!!" Sara joked as she slid across the marble on her white no-show socks, arms outstretched, to give Nate an enthusiastic hug.

"And nothing," Nate said as Sara wrapped her arms around him.

His total surprise was clear from his tone. "Wow! Fantastic! You're naked! Except for the socks," was all he could manage to say. Sara gave him a quick kiss with a slap on the butt before turning and running halfway up the winding staircase.

"You coming, mister?" she asked as she stopped to give her husband a full view. With her palms flat she stretched both of her arms high over her head and gave Nate a wink. She then cocked her head, bumped her butt to the right, turned, and quickly started running, disappearing over the top.

"Man, what a day!" Nate grinned as he ripped the Jerry Garcia necktie from the white Egyptian pinpoint cotton shirt he was wearing. He admitted to himself how lucky he was to still be running after his wife of thirty years.

At first appearance, Nate and Sara Level seemed to have the good life. First impressions, however, often have a dark side.

Chapter 3

A Morning Call

Gordon Manners hit the snooze button on the alarm clock three times before he realized it was a ringing phone. He could have blamed his disorientation on the last shots of liquor he slammed before stumbling to his room and passing out, but instead he blamed the unfamiliar hotel room along with the ungodly hour. Gordon grabbed the landline and pressed it to his ear before falling back into the comfort of the pillows.

"Gordon" was all he could manage to say, his voice painfully reverberating back into his eyes and throat.

"Is this Gordon?" boomed the voice on the other end of the phone.

Before Gordon could answer, the voice came roaring back. "Mr. Gordon Manners of 2122 Louisiana Drive, Houston?"

Gordon's head was pounding as he softly replied, "Yes. This is me." He struggled to open his eyes as he slowly rubbed his temples.

"Mr. Manners, this is Detective Stephen O'Hare over at the Houston Police Department," the voice on the other end of the phone proclaimed. This was followed by a long pause, then he started back up again.

"Mr. Manners, it seems there's been a bit o' trouble down here at your condo," the detective stated matter-of-factly with an Irish brogue.

Gordon grunted.

"There was a robbery, best we can tell. The night watchmen and another man are dead. The door and wall safe were sittin' there wide open when we arrived," the detective said, waiting for a reaction.

After a moment of silence from the other end, the detective continued. "And, well, sir, that wall safe's emptier than a water well in the Sahara."

Gordon managed to sit up on the side of the bed and was fumbling to turn on the light when the detective's voice came exploding back over the phone.

"The security guard is dead along with this other fella. You don't know who this other fellow might be, do ya?" questioned Detective O'Hare.

There was no immediate reaction, so the Detective went on. "Hispanic male, early '30s. Any o' this ring a bell?"

Gordon didn't know how to respond. He was still half in the bag from drinking at the craps table until god knows when. His usual modus operandi was drunk by 10 o'clock or so and asleep (or passed out) by one. Last night the dice gods were favorable, so he drank at the tables until he lost all his earlier winnings. He was guessing he rolled the bones until around three in the morning, but he wasn't positive.

"Mr. Manners, are you still there?"

"Yes, detective," Gordon finally muttered. "I'm just at a loss for words." He punched the illumination on his watch and realized it was 5:30 in the morning.

"You didn't have anybody staying over at your condo last night, now did ya?"

Gordon whispered, "No. No. I... I live alone."

"Well, we didn't' think that was the case. This guy was shot dead in the middle of your living room. Didn't think he was the house sitter. No I.D. Go figure." The detective's voice bounced around in his hung-over brain.

"When are ya getting back in town, Mr. Manners?"

Gordon rubbed his eyes and sighed. "I was planning to stay a couple of days, but I can catch the morning flight back tomorrow... I mean today."

"Good deal, Gordon. Mind if I call you Gordon? Alright. Good deal then. We'll talk soon, Gordon."

"Thank you, detective."

"We'll lock up your condo for ya. Probably need to leave it as a crime scene for the time being. Key was still in the door. You can pick it up when we talk later today. I'll leave my card on the counter here in the kitchen. Call me when you get in and we'll arrange a meet."

Gordon gave no other plan, so the Detective asked, "Gordon, you got any questions?"

Gordon scratched his balls and tried to focus. "How did you find me?"

"Old fashioned police work. Called your office, got your answering service, and right away a Susy Spencer called us back. Told us you were livin' large at the Venetian, out there in Sin City," the detective chuckled. "Las Vegas. See ya later today, Gordon. Right. Okay then?"

There was still no comeback from Gordon, so the Detective wrapped up the call.

"Oh, yea, Gordon. You got quite a mess over here. Might want to call somebody to help ya take care of it. Sorry about the bad news," and Detective O'Hare hung up the phone before Gordon needed to say anything else.

Gordon could not stand up. The instant he slammed the receiver down he began to sweat like he did when he tried to play football in junior high. The sweat pooled under his arms and ran down his forehead. His stomach began to twist. He was going to be sick.

The safe was open and empty. What was in the safe? Gordon expected a call from Santiago. He sat on the edge of the bed and called Susy to have her book the next flight to Houston.

Chapter 4

Plans Change

Tony wasn't quite sure what he was looking at. The two thieves had bolted down the stairs, darted out the back door, and raced two blocks in the rain to where the getaway car was parked. The pair jumped in Tony's old Ford, keeping their eyes glued in the mirror as they drove straight to his apartment without speaking. The getaway was clean. Once safe in the apartment, Jack pulled the two envelopes out from underneath his wet raincoat and threw them on a table. Tony sat down at the table and just stared at them, but unlike Jack, he was still breathing hard.

"Go on, open em' up," Jack ordered.

Tony reached forward, unclipping the metal fasteners securing the envelopes, and poured the contents out onto the linoleum-top table.

"Paper. Just stacks of paper. All this for fucking paper?" Tony was frantic. "Pete died... for this?" Tony fell back in his chair in disbelief. "Pete's dead man." Tony sounded like he was going to cry.

Jack picked up one of the sheets of paper and held it close so he could read it. The paper seemed of good grade, like fine stationery, yet it was thick and coarse. It was brown and green with black type, written in English. He squinted and examined it further. The piece of paper had the number "$50,000.00" typed in the top right corner and the words "World Bank" written in an arch, centered at the top of the page. He read on. *Payable to Bearer Fifty Thousand and no/100 United States Dollars.* Jack thumbed through the stack of paper on the table. They were all the same. Each had the same picture, type, and signature. The only difference was a sequential red number that was stamped in a box at the top left corner of the paper. Inside one of the envelopes was an even smaller one. Jack opened it and poured a computer flash drive out onto the table.

"What the hell?" he thought as he stared at the night's bounty.

When Jack finished examining the packages he looked over at Tony. Tony sat slumped over the table with his arms crossed and his eyes closed. Jack moved around the table behind him. In one fluid motion, Jack grabbed Tony by the hair with his right hand, jerking his head back, and unfolded a knife from his pocket with his left. He ran the cold sharpened steel across Tony's throat in a quick, fluid motion. The blood was immediate, but his death was not. Tony tried to scream but he only gurgled in his own blood. His arms and body shook violently and his eyes stretched wide with shock and disbelief. He gasped, taking in one last look of the world he was about to leave. Jack held onto Tony's hair until the shaking stopped. When he finally let go, Tony fell limp to the tile floor. Jack pulled a cell phone out of his pocket and dialed a number.

"It's me," he said. "Is this still a secure number?"

He nodded and went on, "Yeah, uh huh. Good. Burner cell on this end too."

He wiped the blood off his knife using a clean spot on Tony's shirt. "Didn't have time to take the picture. Plan changed. The wall had a hole in it, wide open, if you get my drift. Ran into an unexpected friend of yours. A professional for sure. He tried to beat the spread. Needless to say, he was taken care of."

Jack listened for a moment, then went on, "You say you've already been contacted about the game? Good. I can leave out the play by play. I traded for a different player. The hole in the wall had hidden treasure." Jack held the phone close to his ear and paced the room.

Gordon Manners was on the other end and said, "You were supposed to steal the painting, Jack. That was the plan."

"Fuck that motherfucking painting! That safe was fucking loaded, Gordon. You can buy the Mona Lisa if you wanted." Jack continued to pace. He wanted to keep all the bonds and pull a double cross. The only reason he couldn't was because he needed Gordon's connection, a reliable fence.

"I don't care what your plan was. There wasn't time. I guarantee you the deal breakers were rolling in the minute I lit off my ten."

Jack bit his lip and flipped his wrist, "Stop your worrying. I took our partner out of the deal and they won't find him till he starts to stink."

"What was in the safe, Jack?" Gordon asked.

Jack laughed, "Bearer bonds issued by the World Bank. Fifty grand each, all matured. There was also a flash drive."

Gordon's voice got higher, "How many bonds are there?"

Jack held back. "Haven't added them all up yet, about two inches worth."

"That wasn't what I hired you for, Jack."

"Now, you listen here hotdog. That stranger offed Pete and I was next in line. He was doing something with those bonds and my guess is that he wasn't gonna share with ya. Now me on the other hand, my momma always taught me to be nice to strangers, respect my elders, and share my toys. So I will, if you're nice," Jack hissed.

"I'm flying back to Houston this morning. I have to meet with the cops. Some O'Hare character from the HPD. It won't take long. Let's say we meet up after that, early afternoon."

"Good choice, we're still partners. You handle the cops. Hell, should be easy for ya, you're clean. I'll head on down to Galveston as planned. I'll be staying at the Tremont Hotel on the Strand. Call me on this number when you're on your way." And with that, Jack hit the end button on his phone and headed for the rendezvous.

Jack was fixated on the bonds as he drove down to Galveston that morning. He kept adding up the number of bonds in his head, then dividing that number by different discount rates. He estimated that the face value of the bonds were worth over $20 million. He knew they'd have to take a lot less to get cash for them in a hurry and stay off the radar.

He was proud of himself and thought out loud, "Damn good day's work. Hell yeah!" Jack slapped the steering wheel as he drove.

The one thing he knew for sure, he was going to play this one close to his vest.

Chapter 5

Old Habits

Nate Level woke up the next morning in quite the good mood. And why not, he thought as he rolled naked out of bed. He had life by the short hairs! He (unlike some of his peers) actually loved his wife, his two boys were finally on their own (for the most part), he had made plenty of money, his investments were solid, and, dammit, his health was pretty good, too.

Nate worked as a partner in the law firm of Manners & Level, Attorneys at Law. Eight years ago, Nate had seen the writing on the wall when Tort Reform was passed by the Texas legislature and as a result dried up all that easy personal injury money. Nate didn't complain about the spilled milk though, his glass was half full. Fortunately, he had already made his money by trying case after case in the courtrooms of Houston, Galveston, and other counties throughout Texas along with federal cases throughout the states. Instead of breaking him, as Tort Reform had done to so many other personal injury attorneys, Nate was given a good excuse to cash out of his old firm, Tanner, Level, Baker & Garth, L.L.P. Unlike most of the other partners, Nate had banked his money throughout the years and could afford to leave the security of the big firm. After he cashed out his share of the assets, he started a small solo shop and changed his brand of law. This proved to be another successful combination.

Back in the heyday when Nate was banging newsworthy verdicts out of juries, the work was his master. The courts and clients dictated his every hour. They dictated when he could sleep, eat, play, have sex, or try to relax. The work told him where he had to be and when he had to be there every day of this life; the practice of law was a jealous, fickle mistress. The courts set his schedule, the clients dominated his time, and the work was never-ending. Always demanding, always on the fast track. The work even told him how to dress and how to act. It got so hectic that at one point he had to hire one employee fulltime just for scheduling. His time had not been his own. It was only after he stopped working 24/7 in the firm and stepped away from the edge of self-destruction that he realized how bad it had actually been. He had lost twenty-five years of his life in a money-induced fog. He was a typical workaholic.

Nate had paid the high price of success. For the most part, he had missed his two boys growing up, his wife growing older, and the real fun from the fruits of his labor. Back in the day, he was always too busy or obsessed with work and his personal life suffered. He wondered now what had driven him so hard.

Nate was the only child of a single working mother growing up without the benefits of money. He didn't know they were poor, let alone how poor they were, until he left the small town of Blessing, Texas, and realized what the rest of the world had to offer. His mother was dead now, but she had always told him the only thing someone couldn't take away from you was an education. So Nate got one. He had worked his way through college by cleaning up the cafeteria behind the rich kids at Southwestern University, an affluent small private school in Georgetown, Texas, which he attended on a work program. He worked construction jobs during the holidays and summers and applied for every grant and loan he could get his hands on. He graduated with a degree in Business/Economics and went right to work for the major construction companies. It was on one of the construction jobs where he met his wife, Sara. He says it was love at first sight. She giggles and says it was more like lust at first glance. They were married soon after.

Sara put Nate through law school working as a sales representative in a software company in their fifth year of marriage. After Nate graduated, he went to work with a vengeance, like his very soul depended on it, chasing the almighty dollar. He forgot to look up for twenty-five years.

He had all the toys and benefits from his labor and all he wanted to do now was to slow down and enjoy life. It was better late than never. He officially got out of the "Banging it out in the courtroom business" and started practicing solo. His solo career lasted a few years, but he didn't like being on his own. Too much administrative work.

He finally settled in with one new partner, Gordon Manners. Gordon had approached him at a symphony fundraiser and the details just fell into place. Their new boutique law firm handled the legal needs for very affluent clients and prosperous businesses. It was no-brainer work for Nate, which was mostly handled by the younger, hourly attorneys and competent legal secretaries. The formula was working. Less stress, more free time, and the money was still rolling in. Billable hours.

On this particular morning, Nate arrived at the office early, at around seven o'clock. He started the forty-minute commute, as usual, pulling out of his driveway in the commuter car, the Yukon 4X4. As he pulled out, he stopped abruptly. He pulled back in, ran upstairs, kissed Sara again, and grabbed the keys to the '65 Mustang convertible. Soaring down the road with the top down brought back old memories. The Mustang was the first car he had ever owned. He bought it for $500 that he had saved up from washing dishes after high school at the Holiday Inn. Nate and his buddies dubbed it the "chick mobile" back before he was married.

He had kept this car all these years and had it fully restored after his youngest son, William Kent Level, ran it into a stop sign. His oldest, Nate Jr., had done significant damage to it as well. They both had been allowed to drive it on special occasions. The one incident Nate always remembered was the morning he was leaving for work and happened to glance over at the Mustang. He saw the spare tire had been put on, the front right quarter panel was annihilated, the driver's door was in the back seat, and there was no hood. He had just had breakfast with the entire family and no one said a word. When he walked back into the house for some answers, Sara rushed over to him as he came through the front door, stopping him with two hands on his chest and said, "They're alright, nobody was hurt."

The two boys, then 18 and 16, looked down the hall from the breakfast table. The youngest tried to smile as the oldest looked like he was about to run for his life. Sara, by then, was tugging at the back of his suit coat, the silent signal for him to shut up and leave. Nate retreated, giving the boys the thumbs up, saying, "Nobody hurt. All's well that ends well. The car can be fixed." He surrendered, turned back around, and went to work. He never quite got the facts of that story straight. Another Mom-and-Son conspiracy.

Nate worked for about an hour in his corner office, reading through some paperwork on a new offshore company the firm had just set up. It wasn't the glamour of trial work, but the flip side was he could do this kind of work from anywhere in the world, so long as he had a computer and email. Free, free, free at last.

Around eight o'clock Gordon Manners' secretary, the person who really ran the business, walked into his spacious office. Her name was Susy Spencer and she had worked for Gordon for fifteen years. Nate had been practicing with Gordon for two. Susy always looked good, smelled like citrus, and cut right to the chase.

As soon as she walked in she said, "Why are you here so early?"

"Old habits die hard," Nate replied. "Besides, I need to talk to Gordon about this trip to Ecuador. Do you know where he is?"

Leaving out Las Vegas and the earlier call from the police, she bit the side of her cheek and said, "At this hour? Definitely in bed."

"Yeah, but whose bed and where?" Nate chuckled.

They both made eye contact. Susy shrugged her shoulders and as she turned to leave said "Let me find him. I'll have him call you as soon as I do." She knew where her bread was buttered and always cover Gordon's ass.

Nice ass for a 48-year-old, Nate thought as he watched her walk out of his office.

Ten minutes later, Susy buzzed him over the intercom, "Gordon's on line 4." Nate reached over and took the call.

"Morning, Gordon," Nate said with a smile.

Chapter 6

Red Eye

Gordon Manners had never flown an early morning red-eye in his entire life. But anything before 10 A.M. was a red-eye in Gordon's eyes. If it wasn't for the importance of this meeting, he would still be in his suite at the Venetian or sitting at a blackjack table with a Bloody Mary. He didn't trust Jack and he knew the sooner he got his cut sorted out, the better. But a cut of what?

Gordon had grown up in the posh Houston suburb of River Oaks. His father had made a fortune in the oil business as a wildcatter before moving from the dirt in Midland to the lights of Houston. His parents were simple country folk who had hit it big and moved to enjoy the high life and everything the city had to offer. They settled on a big house in the close-in, exclusive neighborhood, complete with a private golf course and country club. His father claimed it wasn't for the prestige of the exclusive address, but because it was an easy drive into downtown on what he called "his own private highway," named Memorial Drive. Only the wealthiest Houstonians lived in River Oaks and the county built them a six-lane thoroughfare that they could access from the main street in the neighborhood straight into downtown. After moving to Houston, his father continued to increase his oil fortune and, with his wheelbarrows full of money, moved into real estate. Right time, right place. His daddy hit it big yet again.

Gordon was a child of fortune. Although he went to the finest private prep schools, once he graduated from high school he came to the bitter realization that he could barely read or write. Even at an early age he always made his way through life on his good looks, his suck-up attitude, and Daddy's money.

After high school, he attended the most expensive private college in Texas: Southern Methodist University, which his father had to buy his way into (a pattern Gordon grew accustomed to). In college, Gordon paid other students to do his work. He bought his term papers and essays, he plagiarized, he cheated on exams, yet he still managed to graduate with a degree in sociology. Some attest to the fact that he had a picture of the Dean of the Sociology Department, who was married, smoking a joint with two naked co-eds. Blackmail fit Gordon's style like a glove, it was almost certainly true.

After Gordon purchased his undergraduate degree, his father bought him a condominium on the promise that he would work in the family real estate business.

His father preached, "Start in the mailroom and work your way up in life. It beats the oil patch in the hot Texas sun, boy. And you get to keep all your fingers to boot." This was the plan anyway.

Gordon, however, refused to work. Everyone at the office was afraid of him and he knew it. He was the rich kid whose father owned the company. He never hesitated to let everyone know who his father was, as if they didn't already. He threatened, he complained, he bullied, and he towered over everyone. Everyone at the office worked hard… to stay out of Gordon's way.

The old adage "Don't shit where you eat" proved to be Gordon's downfall. One day he quit working altogether. He didn't even bother to come into the office anymore. After six months of being a no-show, a secretary, who Gordon had jilted, ratted him out to his father. His father was furious and cut him off. But with the constant pressure from his mother, coupled with her influence over his father, Gordon's exile didn't last long.

Gordon realized school was easier than work, so he enrolled at his alma mater with his mother's blessing and attended law school. No one was quite sure how he passed the entrance exam (most who knew him said he didn't), but the school accepted him right around the time they had received a very generous donation. At this stage of his life, Gordon believed his own bullshit and intended on buying another degree. School was not a challenge for Gordon. He paid the other students, cheated on the tests, and blackmailed every professor who showed an ounce of opposition. How he passed the Texas Bar was anyone's guess, but once this hurdle was jumped he hung up his shingle. Gordon Manners, Attorney at Law. Through his parents' businesses, his parents' connections, and his parents' money, Gordon got the clients and then paid other attorneys to do the work. He never missed a social event or an easy mark. This system just worked for him.

Gordon never married nor even had a steady lady. The single life was one by choice. He rented women by the hour in his younger years because of necessity. Later in life he paid them daily rates and kept them for as long as he wanted, or until even all the money he paid them wasn't worth it anymore. These days he would simply drag them drunk out of the strip joints, pick them up in the red light district off Telephone Road, or find desperate waitress types in the diners and lure them in with the promise of easy money. He preferred it better this way.

Dear Daddy died when Gordon was in law school. Gordon didn't miss him. Manners Senior had left millions in real estate, oil wells, and cash. His mother turned out to be a frugal woman, but to Gordon's misfortune, she lived a long life, remarried, and traveled the world first class. Her final illness was treated in the best hospitals at the Medical Center in Houston. When the doctors told her she had less than a year to live, she traveled from Sweden to Argentina, spending money like her life depended on it, looking for that magical cure. She died when Gordon was forty-four. By the time Gordon was fifty-three he had spent his inheritance and was desperate for an easy payday. Insurance fraud with the theft of the Picasso, his last big asset, was his best option. But that was before he learned about the bearer bonds.

The theft of the Picasso was Gordon's grand scheme. He found Jack through his criminal clients and soon after their introduction, the robbery was planned. Gordon had Jack convince the security guard, Pete, and soon to be drinking buddy, that it was his idea. They knew that if Pete had easy access to the condo the temptation for him to steal the Picasso and make some easy money would be too much for him to bear. So they baited him.

Jack instilled the idea in Pete by saying, "If we can just get a copy of that condo key. Talk about an easy payday."

Gordon dropped his keys in the lobby several times, but Pete never snapped. Finally, Gordon got off the elevator late one night and spotted Pete. He acted drunk and knocked over a planter to get his attention. The ceramic pot shattered and dirt went everywhere. He dropped his keys in plain sight and stumbled out the door.

Once Pete made a copy, he was all in. He believed he was the mastermind. After Pete was on board, Gordon had Jack round up another petty criminal; to do the heavy lifting and to make it look like a more complex heist. The two recruits didn't know Gordon was involved.

The painting was the last of his inheritance, and it was insured for millions. Gordon's plan was to collect the insurance money after the theft, along with the cash from the sale of the Picasso on the black market. Jack was promised a percentage from the sale, and Jack and Gordon had agreed to cheat the other two co-conspirators. The safe was not the planned target. In reality, it didn't even belong to Gordon. He was, so to speak, merely renting it out, and he wasn't privy to what was in it.

The safe, along with its contents, belonged to Santiago Valenzuela. It was part of a deal the two had agreed upon in exchange for Santiago paying the mortgage on the condo and sending all his legal business to Gordon. He would get the legal work done, as usual, by referring it out to other, more competent attorneys. This arrangement assured Gordon a steady flow of cash and that his mortgage was being paid down. In return, Santiago gained a safe house and a place to stash valuables. Santiago had the safe installed years earlier, kept a key to the condo, and sent somebody by four to six times a year to stash or retrieve whatever it was they were putting in there. Gordon didn't even know the combination. It was a good deal, one that he didn't want to refuse at the time.

After the phone conversation with Jack, Gordon knew this was one meeting he would not be late for. Ecstatic, he sat in the suite at the Venetian scratching his ass and pouring another shot of Bailey's Irish whiskey into his coffee.

"What was in the safe?" Gordon asked, while his hangover subsided from the ingestion of more alcohol. He planned on bluffing his way through this dilemma much in the same way he lived his life. This was one meeting he would take the red-eye for.

Chapter 7

First-Class Trip

The 747 touched down in San Jose, Costa Rica at around 2:15 p.m. Nate was on it. Earlier that morning, Gordon Manners had been persuasive and promised Nate a two-day turnaround.

Gordon had closed the deal after receiving a text from Susy on his way to McCarran, the Vegas Airport. He was drinking a Bloody Mary in the back of a private shuttle (compliments of the hotel for consistent losers) when he got her message. It read "You were right again. Nate seems willing to go. He'll need convincing. He's in the office. Wants you to call ASAP."

Gordon dialed Nate and pleaded, "Back in Houston in time for dinner the next day, deluxe accommodations and one night of serious fun… Come on, Nate, what are partners for? I know it's last minute, but something's come up. Like we discussed, I can't make it. You can tell me all about it when you get back. Besides, it will be good for you to put a face to all the money they spend with us."

Gordon cast the line by painting a picture. The clients that Nate would be flying to meet picked you up from the San Jose airport by way of a chauffeured limousine. The limousine then drove you to a private airstrip where the corporate jet flew you to their 915,000-acre exotic ranch south of Manta, Ecuador. Gordon explained they did it this way to avoid customs, unwanted delays, and because it was definitely a faster, more reliable way to travel. The plane touched down on their airstrip at the ranch.

"Wait till you get a load of that Lear jet. First class baby!" Gordon set the hook.

Gordon then went on to describe the two-story, stucco hacienda with a red tile roof and long porches with views overlooking the Pacific Ocean. The driveway, front entrance, walkways, and verandas all lead to a rambling pool, all laid in polished red terrazzo tile. The entire compound was surrounded by banana plants, palm trees, and manicured grass laced with exotic flowers. Gordon swore it was right out of the fabulous lifestyles of the rich and famous.

Gordon convincingly reeled Nate in. Upon arriving, there would be a short meeting with the client, Santiago Valenzuela, his concierge, and three business associates. The meeting itself was to discuss the corporate structure of their numerous businesses in the States and should take less than three hours. Nate was more than comfortable with the legal end. He had worked on these corporations for over a year and was familiar with their intricacies. The companies were a tangled web of U. S. Corporations, Limited Liability Partnerships, and Limited Liability Corporations, all of which had offshore partners. Nate had billed these companies a small fortune during the past year alone.

To net the catch and get Nate to agree to go, Gordon finally said, "Shit, I've kissed their ring for over seven years now. It's your turn to put the lipstick on and get your game face ready. Besides, you can bill five hundred an hour for the travel time, the meeting, and while you're lying out by the pool that's full of thong-clad Latina beauties. Come on Nate, do a buddy a favor."

Gordon begged, "It's a no brainer."

Nate let out a dry chuckle, "Fine. You got me. I'll go."

At the conclusion of the conversation that morning, Nate stood up from behind his executive desk and walked into the inner sanctum of the office. This space was better known to the staff as the partners' nap room. It was beautifully decorated with dark oak walls, overstuffed leather furniture, and soft lighting. This room was far different from the rest of the neon-lit workspace and off limits to everyone except Nate and Gordon. His overnight bag was kept in the inner sanctum and had everything he needed for a last-minute trip. There was a dark grey suit, two starched white shirts, and the proverbial red power tie. The carry-on held all the essentials, from a razor to clean underwear. He grabbed the bag and leaned over to push the intercom button.

"Susy, call me a cab to go to George Bush Airport. No, never mind about the cab, I'll take the Mustang. I drove it in this morning. And change Gordon's San Jose reservation to mine."

Susy smirked. She had already changed the flight arrangements yesterday.

Nate thought for a second as he held the intercom button. "And arrange for someone to drive the Mustang from the airport back to my house."

Susy spoke back out of the speaker. "You'd better hurry if you're going to make that flight."

When Nate exited the plane at the Costa Rica airport three and a half hours later, the change in climate was unmistakable. He thought he knew humid having lived in Houston, but as he walked across the tarmac headed toward the small terminal, the rainforest humidity mixed with jet fumes and heat made it hard to draw even a single breath.

Nate entered the terminal and immediately spotted a small Incan-looking man wearing a black chauffeur's hat and holding up a sign that read "Gordon Manners." Nate approached the man, hand extended, explaining that he was the person the sign was looking for. He was met with a limp, wet, dishrag handshake, the kind Nate always took as a sign of weakness. The driver offered him a rotten-toothed smile and the quick understanding that this man neither spoke nor understood English. With a quick burst of Spanish spoken by the driver that went in one ear and out the other, the Incan turned and headed toward the street with Nate in tow. Nate followed the man as he walked out the front doors of the airport, stopping at a black stretch limousine being loaded with his luggage.

Nate thought, "No kidding. This is going to be a hoot."

Nate had not ridden in many limousines and as the plush living room of a car pulled out of the airport, he found it easy to relax. He quickly discovered the mini bar behind the driver's seat and opened an ice cold bottle of Imperial Cerveza, the local beer of choice. He then sorted through a rack of CD's and popped in the Rolling Stones. "Gimme Shelter" cranked through a sound system comparable to the one in his living room.

"I wonder what the poor people are doing?" Nate joked with himself under his breath. He took a long pull off his beer, stretched out his legs, and kicked his shined black Cole Haan wingtips up on the seat beside him.

Nate was finishing off his second beer to the sound of "Street Fighting Man" when the limo turned off the asphalt street and onto a gravel road. The car ripped down the road, throwing a cloud of dust in its wake. As it did, the little Incan turned and gave him a grin, again highlighting the man's gross lack of dental hygiene.

Nate asked, "Is this the way to the airstrip?"

There was no response from the driver.

Nate asked again, "Say driver, how much longer till we get to the jet?"

Still no response.

Nate put his hand on the driver's shoulder through the privacy window and gave it his best shot in Spanish.

"Como se llama?" Nate asked the driver his name in Spanish.

"Me llama Blackie Sancudo," he replied.

"His name is the Black Mosquito? Well, it kind of fits," Nate said to himself. He sat back and listened to the sound of gravel keep time with the music, and watched as the tropical greenery that most people only see on the National Geographic channel rolled by.

Less than an hour after the limo left the airport in San Jose, it abruptly screeched to a halt. As the dust cleared, Nate saw two other cars with their high beams on. One was a blue Lincoln Town Car and the other a late-model Crown Victoria.

"Este es un Aeropuerto?" In broken Spanish, Nate asked if this was the airport.

"Get out of the car!" the Incan ordered as he exited the driver's seat.

"What?" Nate set his beer down and took his feet off the seat. As he sat up he wrinkled his brow and squinted to get a better look out of the window.

"Out of the fucking car, gringo," the Incan said as he walked to the back and jerked open the rear door.

Nate sat there in silence. Before he could say anything, the Incan grabbed him by the lapels of his suit and jerked him out of the limo, shoving him in front of three men standing beside the Lincoln.

In broken English, the Hispanic man standing in front firmly stated, "This isn't Gordon Manners."

The Incan came back, "He's the one that showed up. Bad luck, I guess."

The three men made a semi-circle around Nate, with the Incan standing in the back. "Who the hell are you?" questioned the Hispanic man.

"Nate Level, Gordon's partner. I was sent to handle the meeting with Santiago Valenzuela. What's going on?"

"You didn't bring our kickback. And while we're at it, why don't you tell me what happened in Mr. Valenzuela's safe." There was a short pause, then at the top of his lungs, "Speak up, big shot!" Nate recognized right away that the man was deadly serious.

Nate hesitated. "I... I don't know what you're talking about. I think there has been a mistake here."

"Yeah, there's been a mistake, lawyer man, and you're the one who made it," the man said as he shoved Nate backward. He then arced his fist high in the air and took a swing. Nate ducked, took a step back, and blocked the punch by crossing his hands in front of his face. The man re-cocked his fist and laughed.

Nate dug his feet into the dirt and sprang forward with a right cross. He beat the man to the punch and made solid contact on the side of his face. He followed through with a left uppercut, landing another blow squarely to the jaw. The man to his left stepped in and jackhammered his fist into Nate's stomach, doubling him forward in pain. Nate rolled with the punch and recovered before a second blow. He came back up with an elbow to the man's jugular, causing him to fall back, choking for air. He then rushed the first man putting both hands behind his neck and rammed a knee into his stomach.

With the first man stunned and the second gasping, Nate made a play for the third, leaving the small Incan for last.

"This one's for Sara," Nate said as he made a quick kick to his balls. He missed, but the man moved back. He lunged forward with both thumbs extended to gouge the eyes. The third man blocked the move and assumed a fighting position, both hands up, weight on the back foot. Nate circled the man, desperately looking for an opening. He threw two left jabs, trying to make an opening for a final blow. Before Nate could finish him off, the Incan ran up from behind and put him in a headlock. Nate tried the basic moves to free himself. He went for the eyes, he threw elbows and tried to bite, but he couldn't break the hold. Teaching his boys to fight flashed into his mind and he tried with all his strength to shake the man off his back. But he was simply outnumbered and couldn't get an advantage.

Nate was at their mercy. They took turns hitting him in the face and body while the Incan held on and smiled.

"That's enough," the first man said, throwing his arms in the air. The three men moved back.

He stepped up to Nate's face. "One more time and one time only. Where's our cut and where is Mr. Valenzuela's property? It's not in your luggage, we already searched that." There was a slight pause. "You show up here without our cut and no answers? You fight back. You got some cojones, I'll give you that."

"I still don't know what the hell you're talking about," Nate gasped as he tried to take a step back. He was stopped in his tracks by the Incan behind him.

"Search him!" the man said before landing another crushing blow to Nate's jaw.

Nate was thrown face first against the car by the two men who had not said a word. They cut away his jacket with pocket knives, flipped him over onto the hood of the car, and ripped open his shirt. They tore his shoes from his feet, pulling Nate off the car face down and into the gravel before stripping off his pants. Nate struggled to no avail. He could feel the hot blood trickle down his face as the two men tore through his clothes, checking each and every seam.

"Nothing's here," the larger of the two men said.

"Does Gordon think this is a fuckin' joke? His boy's of no use to us. Send him a message. Mr. Valenzuela would rip out your fingernails and peel the flesh from your face. Feed you your own testicles. But we don't have the time. You're lucky to die this easy," he said before nodding his head.

On cue, all four men grabbed Nate by the ankles, dragging him feet first and palms down across the gravel. It tore open his face, chest, and hands as he kicked for freedom. The cuts were oozing. They stood him up and turned him toward the Incan who popped open a knife from his pocket. Without hesitation, the Incan drove the knife directly into Nate's stomach. The reality was unbearable as Nate involuntarily screamed at the top of his lungs in gritted agony. As the Incan withdrew the knife, he wiped it clean on Nate's now shredded white shirt. Dressed only in that tattered shirt, the four men turned him around to see his fate. Nate realized he was standing on a ledge at the top of a steep mountainside. Inches from his feet, the slope went straight down. Nate's eyes glazed over as his body went numb from the shock.

What is happening? How is this happening? Is this the way it ends, the way I die? He thought of Sara and the boys.

Nate tried to struggle one last time, but the pain had drained every ounce of strength from his body. The Incan placed his foot in the small of Nate's back. He smiled his rotten-toothed smile and then extended his leg, pushing Nate off the mountainside.

Chapter 8

Backwards

Detective O'Hare sat at his desk and flipped through the photographs one more time. He had been involved in hundreds of murders and robberies throughout his career, but something about this one didn't add up. It was all backwards. A dead security guard without a weapon, who was most likely shot by the dead Latino without a weapon. Both men killed with different guns. The security guard was ousted with a 9mm and the Latino with a ten. The one round in the security guard and the two in the Latino had been placed with professional accuracy. Well trained for sure, perhaps even military training. The bullet holes in the door jam and the sheetrock were from a 9mm, probably from the same gun that killed the guard. Those shots must have been intended for someone. Surely the security guard didn't just stand there and wait for a third round to find its mark. O'Hare's guess was the Latino killed the security guard and then fired two more rounds at other unsuspecting and uninvited guests, only to be killed by one of them. He would wait for ballistics from the slugs and the confirmation of any gunpowder residue from the dead men's hands before drawing any hard conclusions.

"What a mess," O'Hare thought.

Detective Stephen O'Hare wasn't a large man. As the name implied, he was one-hundred percent Irish and proud of it. His flaming red hair had thinned over the years, and age-worn freckles and bad skin topped off his 190-pound frame. He was 59 but still built like a bull. He lived with his wife of thirty-four years in an apartment he received rent-free in exchange for acting as the in-house security guard at night. That suited him just fine. He occasionally received midnight calls about strange noises that usually turn out to be teenagers having sex in the pool after hours. All he had to do was grab his flashlight and scare them away. Easy work for free rent.

It was one in the afternoon, but he had been up since 4 a.m. He was thinking of a chili cheese dog and a cold beer when his phone rang.

"O'Hare," his gravelly voice rang into the phone.

"Yes, detective, this is Gordon Manners."

"Hey, Gordon. You back in Houston?" O'Hare asked.

"Took the first red-eye out. I'm just sitting here in my condo now. I took your advice and called the management company. They promised to get a cleaning crew on this right away."

There was a long deliberate silence from O'Hare.

"Detective, you asked me to call," Gordon said.

"Yea, yea, Gordon. I need to make a report. When can you make it down to the station?"

"Is all that necessary?" Gordon sounded put out.

O'Hare clarified, "Well, you see, I got two stiffs down here. One of 'em was in the middle of your living room, the other at your front door.

Got an empty safe and what they tell me is an expensive painting that was left hanging on your wall. I'd kinda like to get your take on all this."

Gordon sighed, "What about tomorrow morning?"

"Tell you what, I'm getting ready to head out. If you don't mind I could come by your condo in about twenty minutes. Headed out that way anyway."

O'Hare wasn't going to give him a way out. He wanted some explanations before Gordon had time to think too much about it. Gordon didn't seem concerned or surprised and he wanted to see why. Face to face. All the telltales come out when you are one on one. Body language, eye dilation, speech. O'Hare needed to get his story and the sooner the better. He made note of Gordon's hesitation.

"That'd be great. I really appreciate you going out of your way on this. You know this whole thing is rather unnerving for me. I'm afraid I'm not thinking straight, know what I mean?" Gordon said.

O'Hare didn't, but he followed along anyway. "Sure, sure. Protect and serve. You know how that goes. It's no trouble at all. Happy to oblige. I'll see ya in twenty." O'Hare reached across the desk and hung up the phone.

As he leaned back in his chair, O'Hare scratched his head and looked down at the crime scene photos. "That man's a piece of work. Hasn't asked what happened. Hasn't asked who died. Doesn't say anything's missing. If I hadn't personally verified he was in Vegas, I'd bet he was at the condo when the shooting went down. Might still be involved somehow. Too soon to make any conclusions."

Detective O'Hare's new partner was in the bathroom. He knew it was mean, but it was a good opportunity to ditch her. He stood up and headed out of the station, still thinking about that chili cheese dog and a cold Guinness to wash it down.

Chapter 9

Home Run

Gordon sat in the condo, his mind racing. At first he didn't see any problems, but now the alcohol was wearing off and he was becoming concerned. This was a conundrum alright. Gordon wasn't prone to panic and he hadn't spent a great deal of his life worrying about things. As he sat in his condo and looked at the bloodstained carpet, open safe, and bullet holes in the wall, he decided, yes, he was worried. Reality was settling in. Dead people, cops, and that damn secret in the safe. He decided he would wing it. His arrogance told him it would be easy, but just before he convinced himself to calm down, his cell rang.

"Gordon," he answered.

"Where's my property, slick?" The voice on the other end had a heavy Mexican accent.

It was a voice that Gordon recognized immediately. It was Santiago Valenzuela, the owner of the safe. They had only met less than half-a-dozen times over the years. Santiago had come to his office originally to discuss setting up his business entities, the other times he had lavishly entertained

Gordon at his estate in Ecuador. The rest of their business was done by burner phones. Santiago was pure Latino by nature, machismo and all. Gordon had never heard him laugh, tell a joke, or make small talk. He was all serious and never one to waste time.

Over the years, Gordon had paid Santiago hundreds of thousands of dollars in referrals, as the attorneys called it, as part of their arrangement. In addition to billing Santiago $500 an hour, plus expenses, Santiago sent Gordon other clients. Gordon would sign them up and split the attorney fees with Santiago. The money made from the routine cases sent his way were rarely accounted for, but the personal injury settlements were always split between them, with the lion's share going to Santiago. As far as Gordon was concerned, it was free money. He had just received a huge settlement from BP in the Texas City refinery explosion. Santiago sent him two injured laborers and a crying widow. As always, the checks were deposited in offshore bank accounts, the fee was split, and Gordon would drag his cut back stateside, evading taxes however he could. Easy, easy money. Unfortunately, Gordon's lifestyle demanded a lot. Gordon knew that to split fees with non-attorneys was illegal, but he never thought twice about it. He also knew that soliciting clients, or running cases as the attorneys called it, was illegal, not to mention morally reprehensible. But then again, he couldn't give a tinker's damn. Morals were not his strong suit.

Gordon knew Santiago as the head of a major drug cartel that was one of the biggest distributors of coke, heroin, and pot north of the border. Wanted by the FBI. Gordon also knew the risks of dealing with that particular type of client.

"Mr. Valenzuela," Gordon cringed into the phone.

"The last guy who told me he didn't know anything is dead. He said he was your partner. They gave him the benefit of the doubt, so he was treated with respect. Made it fast. You lie and it won't go so good for you, Gordy."

Santiago didn't bluff.

But Gordon saw the opportunity to kill two birds with one stone. This was, after all, a situation he could finesse using his magic charm, something he had mastered throughout years of practice. He needed to find out what was in the safe and get back in good graces with his money machine.

Gordon launched "Just tell me what I need to do to fix this, Mr. Valenzuela."

"Don't even start your high-dollar, silver-tongued bullshit with me, Gordito. Tell me where the envelopes are and you might make it through this with all your limbs intact," Santiago demanded. "Both envelopes, Gordy. The twenty-five mil in bearer bonds and the flash drive. I'll be there personally to pick them up. Stand me up or don't deliver, I'll make sure you live in pain for as long as my doctors can keep you alive. You'll tell me everything I need before I even start, and I'll still make you scream for weeks. Don't play me, pendejo. I'll shit in the mouth of your dead. We'll be seeing each other real soon."

Santiago hung up before Gordon could respond.

Wow! Gordon thought as a broad smile crept across his face. *Twenty-five million.* At last, a home run. The killing part worried him, but once he got his hands on that much cash he'd make like a ghost.

"Poor Nate. What a tool" he said to himself as he pondered what to tell Nate's social princess of a wife. He'd think of something. Maybe a plane wreck? Car crash? Probable. Just as he was spooling over the fate of his partner, the doorbell rang.

"Come on in," Gordon yelled.

The door opened and Detective O'Hare walked in.

Chapter 10

Not Among Thieves

After Jack checked into the four-star hotel in Galveston, he Googled "Backpage" on his iPhone and ordered a chocolate and vanilla duo. When that bored him, he threw a wad of cash on the bed and sent them on their way. As he lay on the bed he started fantasizing about how he was going to spend his newfound fortune. He always wanted a diamond Rolex to replace his cheap Timex. A new sports car would be nice, probably a convertible. Maybe even a Jaguar or a Mercedes.

"Clothes," he said. "Tailor-made suits, silk shirts, robes for leisure around the pool."

Jack snapped his fingers.

"And a new pair of cobra skin cowboy boots and a beaver Stetson. Stylin'." His wants ran rampant but stayed within the confines of his upbringing.

"Oh yeah, this is going to be fun." Jack slapped his thigh in chagrin.

He started retracing his steps as he relaxed on the bed. He had gotten away without a trace. No evidence left behind. After the deed was done, he had carefully showered back at his apartment and thrown the bloody clothes in a dumpster across town. No fingerprints, he had picked up his shell casings, and the witnesses were all dead. Things were looking up.

"Dead men tell no tales," Jack smiled.

"I'll be a ghost in the wind." He liked the way that sounded. "A rich one."

He leaned back and laughed out loud. "Cash the bonds, get my cut, and disappear."

Jack dreamed on.

The last link of physical evidence was the pistol he pinched off the dead Mex and his own. He'd toss them into Galveston Bay after his meet with Gordon. Jack stuffed another pillow behind his head and stretched out on the bed.

"Fuck it," he laughed again. "I'm gonna go get drunk."

With his new mission at the forefront on his mind, Jack wandered out onto the most popular street in Galveston, the Strand. The Strand was one block off the Port of Galveston and in times past served as warehouse space and as the entertainment district for the seamen in port. The old 18th-century red-brick street had been torn up and replaced with asphalt with the exception of the crosswalks, which gave it the taste of a bygone flavor. Over the years, the Strand had turned into a commercial tax base for tourism, lined with souvenir shops, restaurants, and watering holes.

"A Bourbon Street wannabe," Jack spat under his breath.

The tourists proved too much to put up with, so he headed two streets up to an old haunt called O'Malley's. Once inside he settled in at the bar and ordered a shot of Jaegermeister and a rum and Coke. He downed the shot, sipped the rum, and then took out his phone to dial Gordon.

"Gordy, my man. Where ya at?" Jack's mood had lifted. He licked his lips, slowly feeling the liquor.

"On my way to Galveston," Gordon replied. "Should be there in about an hour. Hey, where you at? You at the hotel?"

Jack replied, "No. Decompressing on a bar stool. I'm out havin' an adult beverage. Listen, call me when you hit town and I'll meet you back at the hotel."

Jack was almost excited and exclaimed, "Gordy, we hit the mother lode! We're partners now, right?"

"All in a day's work, amigo. Wait for my call. We'll hook up, work on our exit strategy, and take it from there. We're gonna have to lay low for a couple weeks. It'll take some time, but trust me Jack, we'll be on easy street soon enough." Jack heard a small bell ringing in the background.

"Look forward to it," Jack said, hanging up the phone and ordering another rum drink with a whiskey back.

*   *   *

As the phone call ended, Gordon slipped his black Porsche 911 GT3 up to the valet at the Tremont Hotel and grabbed a crowbar from the hood. He walked to the front desk and handed the clerk a hundred dollar bill in exchange for a key card.

"Mr. Manners." The desk clerk respectfully nodded as he handed Gordon the prearranged key card.

Gordon grabbed the key and told the clerk, "Don't worry, Jerry. No one will ever know you gave me this key. Consider it payback. You still owe me for your daughter's criminal case. Right?"

The desk clerk answered, "Yes sir, Mr. Manners. Just between you and me."

As Gordon turned and headed for the elevator, he thought, *What a chump. His daughter shoplifts a cheap necklace at Wal-Mart and the little man thinks it'll ruin her life. What a waste of my legal talent. One court appearance, a quick plea deal, and he's my bitch for life. Practically gave me a license to steal.* And Gordon did just that every chance he got.

Gordon tossed Jack's hotel room in short order. After all, how many places can you hide something in a hotel room? This wasn't the movies. There was the bed, the drawers, it could be taped under something, in the closet, air duct, or the bathroom. The small safe in the room was still open.

"Damn it! Not here." Gordon shrieked. Jack wouldn't carry the package with him, Gordon was sure of that.

"That only leaves his car," Gordon said as he bolted out of the room.

*   *   *

Jack relaxed at the bar, drinking and patiently waiting on Gordon's call. He was on his fourth rum and third shot when he lit a Camel non-filter and took a long drag.

"Hey buddy, no smoking by city ordinance," the short, balding, four-eyed little whiner in a necktie blurted out from across the bar. Jack just turned around on his bar stool, drink and smoke in hand, and ignored the little pissant. As he took another drag off the cigarette, he gazed out of the bar through a small window and watched the Galveston Train Trolley rumble past.

"Shit!" Jack screamed and jumped to his feet. He threw his cigarette on the floor, reached into his pocket, and tossed a couple of twenties on the bar. The front door of the bar slammed behind him as he ran down 4th Street, hustling the four blocks back to the hotel.

As Jack raced toward the hotel at a full sprint, he realized what was going on. "A double cross. Trust that weasel? What was I thinking? That bell ringing on the phone when I was talking to Gordon was the trolley! Gordon was already here! That whore," he spat.

Jack had relaxed, let his guard down, and was now paying the ultimate price. If Gordon found the package before Jack got his cut, he'd be shit out of luck, screwed, beaten, a loser, and worst of all, still dead broke.

"Over my dead body," he said as he leaped off the curve and dodged around traffic heading down the street.

Jack ran at an all-out sprint toward the hotel as his chest lit on fire and the adrenalin pumped through his every muscle.

*   *   *

Gordon stepped out of the elevator and walked across the street to the covered three-story garage used by the Tremont Hotel to park cars. He knew Jack's car. It was a jalopy Jack had hopped up with old-school V8 muscle. Gordon would recognize the junker right away. As he trotted up from the first floor searching the garage, the parked cars became a pattern of relatively new millennium mobiles. There was your standard Lexus, the Nissans, the Hondas, the low-end Mercedes, and sometimes even an occasional high-dollar pickup or SUV. One floor before Gordon made it to the roof and just as he was starting to wonder if this would work out for him, there it was. Jack's 1976 rusted Plymouth.

"Bingo." Gordon was smitten with himself.

He smashed the window with the crowbar and quickly looked in the cab. Nothing. He popped the lock on the trunk, lifted it open, and threw back the matt covering the spare tire. Gold at the end of a rainbow: two manila envelopes lying under a sawed-off shotgun with a pistol grip and a handgun with a silencer. He grabbed the packages and stuffed them in his pants under his sports jacket, then grabbed the shotgun and jacked a shell into the chamber. Two stories down then across the street to his Porsche and he would be home free with the bonds; no partner and he still had the Picasso.

"Home run, baby!" Gordon almost pissed himself with joy. He turned to make the dash to his Porsche, thinking only of the riches and how smart he was.

As he pivoted he was stopped dead in his tracks by the reality of a cold steel barrel pressing directly against his forehead.

"Whoa, whoa, Jack. Slow down, partner," Gordon pleaded, putting both hands in the air, one clutching the shotgun. Jack did a quick search and grabbed the packages, the gun never leaving Gordon's forehead.

Jack said in a slow out-of-breath drawl, "What now, Gordy?"

"Wait, Jack. This isn't what it looks like. I was going to give you the Picasso. No bullshit. It's in the Porsche, Jack. It's parked in front of the hotel." Gordon was thinking as fast as he could, trying to come up with a new scheme.

"I needed to know what exactly was in those packages before I approached you with this idea," Gordon said.

"Keys," Jack demanded as he pushed the gun harder into Gordon's forehead.

Gordon negotiated, "Hey, let's just take a second, and talk this through."

"Now!" Jack barked, grinding his teeth as he extended an open callused hand.

Jack's newfound plan was solid. He knew what he was going to do. His best option was to take the keys to Gordon's Porsche, stuff Gordon in the trunk of the Plymouth, put a bullet in his head, and get the hell out of Galveston with the bonds. The Plymouth wasn't registered in Jack's name anyway and he knew Gordon's car was registered under the dealer's name. If the Picasso was in Gordon's car, so be it. If it wasn't, screw the lying little soon-to-be corpse. Jack had the bonds. He would find a way to sell them on his own. Either way, it was a win-win.

Jack hit Gordon with the pistol as hard as he could. Gordon fell back into the trunk of the car, and a single shot rang out from the shotgun he was holding. As he slammed into the floor of the trunk, Gordon's face squinched tight, waiting on Jack's final bullet. When nothing followed, he slowly raised his body off the floor of the trunk and looked over the tailgate. He saw Jack down on one knee. Blood and meat were splattered on the concrete from where the accidental shotgun blast had made a direct hit on what was now Jack's mangled leg. Jack's gun was laying in the blood while his thigh squirted blood on it, heartbeat by heartbeat, like a child pulling the trigger on a water gun. Gordon was dazed, but he climbed out of the trunk and kicked the gun away from Jack's grasp. Gordon grabbed the packages off the ground, staring at the dark red carnage as the kneeling Jack fell face forward onto the bloody concrete. Gordon checked for any witnesses. The parking garage was empty. He looked back in the trunk, grabbing the silenced pistol and shoving it in his pants. He took one more look at Jack's still body, turned, and walked down the garage ramp, heading to his Porsche. Gordon was elated, thinking only of himself and his loot.

As Jack lay on the third floor of the parking garage, sprawled out in a pool of his own blood, the shock and adrenaline took over. He rolled over, sat up, and ripped his shirt off, tying it around his thigh for a tourniquet. As the bleeding subsided he dragged himself over to the pistol and picked it up. He forced himself off the concrete and into the driver's seat of the

Plymouth. Leaning over, he popped the glove box and downed a handful of his recreational oxy.

Jack focused, "It ain't over till it's over." He started the V8 muscled, "That son of a bitch is going to pay."

When Jack put the car in reverse the tires screeched as they slid across the fresh blood. He slammed it into drive and drove out of the garage, the tires echoing at every turn while the trunk banged up and down, open and closed. As he drove down the street, he spotted Gordon's Porsche four blocks up, turning left.

Chapter 11

Keep Your Head On

Detective O'Hare sat behind his desk at the station talking to himself and eating a fast food salad. The rest of the department was wise enough to stay out of his way when the mumbling (as they called it) started. His new partner, Gini Gibbs, found this habit rather odd and was sneaking up behind the detective to listen to the old man's conversations with himself. The rest of the department was, of course, well versed in the dangers of what happened when you crossed the legendary O'Hare. Despite his odd ways, he was the most decorated, straight-shooting, case-solving, methodical sloth in the whole department. When stuck or stumped on a losing case, everyone in the department turned to O'Hare for advice. His new trainee, as O'Hare called her, was too green to know any better. Gini would learn quick not to get too personal with O'Hare or else she would find herself back in traffic, or worse, the basement. And that was just how things worked. His wit seemed slow and unimposing at first, yet it struck the bull's eye like an ax driven into hardened oak.

"A salad, huh?" O'Hare mumbled. "Okay. So what if I bought it at McDonald's? It's still a salad."

"What do you mean I need to eat more salads?" he said reliving a conversation he had earlier with his wife.

"Something about a pot and a black kettle," he mumbled, recalling his response.

"Oh, yeah. Right. My health is your only concern?" O'Hare muttered as he played with the salad.

"Jesus woman, I'm in the gym before daylight at least three days a week. The workouts aren't the same, but I'm sweating, hittin' the bag on occasion, working the machines, swimming, then taking a long steam. Just look at the other guys my age." His wife always knew the right old man buttons to push.

"I'm eating the salad! Be proud of me at least, woman. They had the Big Macs, home-style burgers, fries, shakes, and I got the salad! I could have gone across the street for the ultimate cheeseburger," he continued talking to himself as he stared at the salad and squeezed more Thousand Island dressing on it in a futile attempt to get any kind of taste experience. He missed, leaving a sizeable stain on his shirt.

"Come on, honey, really? More salads?" O'Hare muttered as he licked the salad dressing off his shirt.

Just when Gini realized how much ammunition she had to properly tease O'Hare, the phone rang. She ran over and grabbed it.

"O'Hare's desk. Yes, he's in," she said before handing O'Hare the phone. With a flip of his finger, O'Hare launched the plastic spork across the desk and answered the phone.

"O'Hare," he stated. "Ah, good to hear from you, Kempy. How's the sheriffin' business down there?"

Brian Kempel, nicknamed "Kempy," was a sheriff in Galveston County. In most cases, law enforcement agencies in South Texas jurisdictions didn't share information or much less give a rat's ass about the cases that aren't in their own counties. Although Galveston County bordered Harris County, the two counties refused to cooperate with each other out of rivalry. Galveston was fun in the sun, party central, and tourist friendly. Houston, a model of law and order that was tough on crime, cowboys, and big oil. The two rivals were as different historically as they were politically. Fortunately, the two men now on the phone together were from the old school and couldn't care less about the rivalry, power, or political control. They were what the departments called "real cops."

O'Hare made a clicking sound between his teeth "You don't say. Could be. Yea, big coincidence if it's not. I know where it is. Green's Island Diesel right after the causeway bridge. See you in about forty-five."

With that, O'Hare tossed the salad in the trash can, making a metal tang sound and headed out with Gini trailing behind.

"Where are we going?" Gini asked.

"Galveston," O'Hare responded, "after a quick stop at Pappas BBQ. You hungry?"

Gini did not respond.

After a stop at the BBQ drive-thru, O'Hare and Gini headed to Galveston. Gini wasn't hungry and watched O'Hare wolf down a sliced beef sandwich while driving 95 mph down the interstate with one knee. Gini wondered if she should hand him a napkin or just reach over and wipe the BBQ sauce off his already stained shirt. She decided to let sleeping stains lie. After crossing the causeway bridge onto the island, they pulled into the heavy equipment repair yard, better known as Island Diesel. As the two rolled to a stop in the dusty parking lot they saw Kempy and his partner talking to the owner, Bob Green. They were standing next to a gargantuan Caterpillar D10 bulldozer and a boom crane that made the Sheriffs' cruiser look like a Hot Wheel.

The owner, Bob Green, was a colorful character whose reputation preceded him. Both Kempy and O'Hare knew him and despite his shenanigans from Galveston to Houston, and for that matter throughout South Texas, if you could get Bob to fix your car, boat, toys, or other floating or rolling stock, you considered it a win. Bob only wanted to repair the big machines, but he was always up for a "fix your buddy's shit day" and after a little bit of wrangling he'd repair anything you asked with a cagey smile. Of course, he expected reciprocation in kind and in Bob's world, the cops always played a leading role. No telling when you'd need a favor from a cop was Bob's philosophy. Just a matter of time. Not if, but when.

O'Hare watched the two shake hands, then Bob retreated back into the air-conditioned shop. Kempy turned and approached O'Hare's cruiser as he rolled the window down. The humidity hit the inside of the car like a sauna. Gini ran her fingers under her collar.

Kempy leaned in the window, gesturing as he explained, "The car wreck is on the other side of this bulldozer. You can't see it from here, but as I said on the phone, I'm pretty sure you need to see this one with your own two eyes." Kempy stood up and took a step back from the cruiser.

O'Hare nodded as the sheriff continued, using his hands as he always did when he spoke. "Forensics and the medical examiner are still about an hour out. So go ahead and knock yourself out, just don't do anything stupid like hurt yourself," he looked over at Gini, then back at O'Hare. "There was a pistol in the cab of the car. Blood all over it. It's in an evidence bag in what's left of the trunk. A shotgun is lying there, too. Found it in the trunk."

Kempy shrugged as he extended his right hand through the car window. O'Hare shook it, exited the car, and walked around to the front of the 24-foot D10 dozer. Gini scurried behind him, wondering why anyone in the world would choose to retire in this god-forsaken climate as the sweat began to trickle down the small of her back.

When she caught up to O'Hare he was already examining the twisted pile of blue metal that was once a car. The heap of jagged rubble was halfway under a 16-foot yellow bulldozer blade attached to a machine so big she had only seen one once on TV. The car had obviously run directly into the front of the dozer, with the blade shearing the roof clean off. The blade of the dozer had been about three feet off the ground at the time of impact, which resulted in the decapitation of not only the roof of the car but the driver as well. The result was unmistakable. The roof of the car had been shaved and folded back like an accordion when the car passed under the blade and then slammed to a stop when it smashed into the front of the earthmover itself. Part of the engine was now in what was left of the passenger seat. The top of the car had been peeled off and folded all the way back to the rear window, essentially making the four-door hardtop a convertible. The trunk lid was standing wide open. A headless driver was sitting in the front seat. O'Hare took mental notes as he watched Gini climb in and out of the wreck.

O'Hare watched Gini lean in behind the blade for a closer look. "Not as much blood as I would expect," she said.

"Seen a lot of headless drivers in your career?" O'Hare asked.

"First one, smart ass. Still, sever the carotid artery in one fell swoop and the blood should flow out like Niagra. Are we missing something here?"

O'Hare responded, "Just all the facts."

Detective O'Hare picked up the evidence bag out of the open trunk and studied the weapon. A 10-millimeter Colt combat automatic. He looked down at the shotgun. *What are the odds? This pistol had to be the same one used in the robbery and murder in that attorney's condo. Had to be,* he reasoned.

As he considered the odds, O'Hare wondered if he could get away with stopping at the dog track on the way back to place some off-track bets on the ponies. He looked at Gini and thought to himself, *No way. College girl is a sweaty mess. Not a bad call about the blood though.*

O'Hare walked over and gave Kempy his thanks. They both knew the odds of this pistol not being the one that was used in the Houston murders. A 10mm automatic was not your average criminal's everyday weapon.

"The department leaks like an old barn roof," O'Hare told Kempy. Everyone knew about the facts, they were all over the papers after all.

Kempy knew the consequences, "Makes it hard to do an interrogation or keep the wackos from confessing. Positive side is I knew to call you."

O'Hare took another look at the wreck and turned again to Kempy. "Did you get a chance to talk to Mr. Green?"

"Sure did. He didn't see nothin', only heard the noise."

"Hmm. Had he been drinking?"

Kempy laughed, "You know, you can't ever tell with Bob."

O'Hare smirked and replied with "Isn't that the truth." He got in the car and headed back to Houston with Gini in tow.

Chapter 12

Third-World Hideout

Gordon had last seen Jack sprawled in a puddle of his own blood, face down on the concrete. It was over. He wiped away any prints on the shotgun and had thrown it in the trunk of Jack's car. He walked, overconfident, out of the garage as he combed his hair and brushed off his clothes.

The garage was isolated, no one witnessed Jack's last breath, and the shotgun blast had seemingly gone undetected. He let relief wash over him as he spooled over the events. The world was turning his way, it was playing his song. He would soon have enough money to live in the style he deserved. He'd be able to do as he pleased, he'd be set for life. This last triumph was over; he could disappear anywhere in the world and sort out early retirement. The high life of leisure awaited him.

Gordon didn't bother to tip the valet as he slipped into the leather seat of his Porsche. He opened the sunroof and pushed the start button. A new car would definitely be in order. He was upside down on this one anyway, let the dealer repossess it. Luckily, his credit score was of no concern now. Gordon spit out the window and drove toward the first road heading out of

Galveston. As he passed the shipyards, shrimp houses, and factories on the island's north end, he rolled down all the windows and turned up the air conditioning. The faint sound of a train whistle blew in the distance as he slowed down, anticipating his last diversion before leaving the island for good.

Down the road, there was a train stopping traffic as it rumbled down the track. It was commonplace on this part of the island. The black-and-white striped crossing arms fell as the red lights blinked and the bell repeatedly pinged for caution. He pushed on the brakes and put one of his favorite CDs in the player. AC/DC's "Have A Drink On Me" blasted through the speakers as Gordon slipped on his Costa Del Mar sunglasses and waited for the train to pass. He loved it when a plan came together. As he admired himself in the rear view, a slight grin on his face, he caught a glimpse of a small dust cloud headed his way. He adjusted the rearview for a better view and watched it moving down the shoulder, next to the line of cars waiting with him on the train. Inside the cloud, something moved up and down. He turned around in his seat to get a better look and watched whatever it was going up for just a second, then down, disappearing. He saw it, then it was gone. It was moving in the dust cloud and as it got closer he heard a rhythmic *Bang! Bang! Bang!* Gordon was puzzled until it finally got close enough for him to make out what it was.

It was Jack! Now to close for comfort. Gordon would have never noticed him had it not been for the trunk of the car bouncing up and down as Jack soared down the shoulder straight toward him. Gordon was trapped behind the train. When Jack was one car length behind him, Gordon yelled at the train.

"Hurry. Faster. Get the fuck out of the way!"

Three, two, one... Gordon slapped the car into first gear and shot around the railroad guard arms, just missing the rear of the train by seconds. Gordon heard the bang of the trunk and the squeal of tires from behind him. He looked in the mirror. Jack's car was approaching fast, he was going to ram him. Jack was inches from Gordon's bumper as the two rumbled across the tracks. Gordon picked up speed. His car was quicker and he watched himself gain a little distance. When Gordon looked down from the rear view mirror he saw that the distant traffic light was red, the traffic backed up. Gordon was forced to slow down and Jack caught him, ramming into the rear end of his car with a loud smash. The impact threw Gordon backward and then into the steering wheel as he struggled to gain control of the sliding Porsche. He took the only option he had, a road to his right. Gordon floored it, redlined the tack and ground the gears as fast as he could shift. Again, he slowly began to put some distance between himself and Jack. As Gordon went through the gears, he looked down the road. His advantage would not hold out for long. The road was a dead end. It turned into a caliche parking lot surrounding a large metal building. Gordon's car slid sideways as he peeled off the blacktop and shot across the parking lot. He could hear the roaring V8 engine hot on his tail.

Gordon's lost control as he hit the loose caliche. He bit his tongue and tried to control the car as it went into a sideways slide. The flying rocks and white smoke spewed all around him, washing out any clear view. Gordon kept a tight grip on the wheel and worked the gears as his stomach flipped and the taste of acid filled his mouth.

When Jack saw Gordon's car jump from the asphalt onto the gravel parking lot he said, "Got him! I'm gonna put this car right up his ass!" Jack watched Gordon go into a tailspin and he angled the Plymouth straight toward him, full throttle. He kept his foot in the carburetor and T-boned Gordon's driver's door. More gravel and dust burst into the air.

Out of nowhere, Gordon felt the hard impact. He heard the metal on metal smash as his body slammed sideways. He held onto the steering wheel as his car turned a full circle, but somehow he managed to push in the clutch and downshifted.

The impact threw Jack forward and his foot slipped off the gas. When he looked up he was driving blind. The haze was too thick. He didn't care and he didn't let up. The loss of blood along with the oxy created an uncontrollable rage. He slammed the pedal back down and the car picked up speed.

When Gordon heard Jake's engine roar, he was terrified. He struggled with the steering wheel as the car continued to slide. He could feel his heart beating through his neck as he finally regained control and the dust cleared. He surprised himself. Then out of nowhere, he heard a long, loud crunching sound. It startled him so bad that his body jumped unannounced, like someone jumped out, unexpected, from behind a closed door. Gordon looked in his mirror and saw Jack's car buried underneath a big yellow machine. He felt a moment of relief but kept his foot on the gas. He prayed Jack couldn't catch him again or, even better, was dead.

Gordon sped around the building, off the gravel, and back on the blacktop while AC/DC's "You Shook Me All Night Long" cranked out of his stereo.

Gordon's mind raced. Which plan to follow? Lay low in Houston or just take off? There was no way he could go back to his condo. Bad move. It was only now when he realized how he had grossly underestimated Jack and probably Santiago as well. After this escapade, he was through taking stupid gambles with his life. Although he couldn't be sure Jack was dead, he was sure the Mexicans were coming. No doubt about that. Time for his ace in the hole.

Throughout his adult life, Gordon maintained a well-stocked safe house. The place had been sold and re-sold through no fewer than fifteen corporations, all untraceable to Gordon. He always considered it to be located in a third-world country with modern-day amenities.

Gordon's third-world country had a population of around three million, concentrated in and around two cities. The country was big enough to travel around in, at 48,000 square miles, with good roads, sound infrastructure, and modern utilities. English was the spoken language, the American Dollar was the currency, and gambling was legal. To Gordon, this meant he could drink, gamble, and whore in the city, yet it was big enough to hide in the countryside. He could still drive a sports car, have reliable public utilities and didn't have to learn a foreign language or an exchange rate. Gordon's third-world country was, in fact, the State of *Mississippi*, the safe house being just north of Biloxi.

The safe house was located on 250 acres that belonged to his great-grandmother and left to Gordon by default. If it had ever been worth any real money, Gordon would have sold it years ago. After his father's death, Gordon talked his mother into building a new glass and steel house on the property, complete with a bomb shelter. That bomb shelter had been a prime selling point for his mother. It played to her fear of a foreign invasion, a minority revolt, or class warfare. Bless her heart, Gordon still remembered the endless conversations that worried his mother to no end.

"A place to go when the poor folk rise up against the wealthy. You've seen pictures of the slums, those blacks are dangerous." Gordon would roll his eyes. His mother would wring her hands.

"And the damn Russians. They have the nuke." His mother would remember hiding under a desk as a child. Gordon would turn away and mock her.

"It's going to be ugly. We can't stay in the city. Where will we go?" Gordon grew a tree of worry.

"They'll rise up, loot and riot in the streets. It won't be safe. You have to have a bug out plan, Mom," he would go on causing her sleepless nights.

Out of fear, his mother finally succumbed and built a modern house, tearing down Grandma's old clapboard shanty. A third-world country, to Gordon. His perfect hideout. Mom's old family homestead, just north of Biloxi, Mississippi.

Gordon put the new plan in motion, leaving Galveston the back way, across the Bolivar ferry headed to Biloxi. On the ferry, he checked out the damage to the Porsche. He decided it would be all right as long as the tail-lights worked, but he still wasn't sure if he was going to fix it or abandon it altogether. Gordon took a long, deep breath and glanced around the inside of the car.

On the front seat were two manila envelopes and a pistol. In the back was a towel-draped frame. Under the towel was the Picasso.

Gordon was scared for his life, a first for Gordon. He knew now would not be the time to take chances, let alone stupid ones. Santiago was coming. Nate was dead. Jack could still be very much alive, but he would never find him at the safe house. Blame the theft on Nate and let Sara take the bullet.

Chapter 13

The Long Night

The first night Nate was traveling and didn't call, Sara got mad. Nate had phoned her early that morning, while he was on his way to the airport, and told her he was going on that last-minute (yet still expected) business trip. The one he had mentioned to her as he walked out the door on his way to work this morning. He had also mentioned it to her when he came home from work last night but didn't think she was listening. He assured her it was no big deal. He had to fill in for Gordon and go personally. He promised to call when he got there and be home for dinner the next day. She pressed him for more details.

"Where are you traveling to again?"

Nate sighed, "South America. I told you."

"Yeah, when you were walking out the door this morning. And last I checked, South America's a pretty big continent."

"Ecuador," she heard him say over the phone. She could hear the engine of his Mustang roar in the background.

Sara waited in silence for more information, so Nate went on, "I'm sure they have phones. Maybe not reliable cell reception, but there's bound to be a landline somewhere in the country. Look, I'll call you when I land later today. I'm scheduled to be back in Houston tomorrow, late afternoon. Should be just enough time for me to take my awesome, wonderful, very understanding wife out to a nice dinner."

Sara responded, "Ha! We'll see. You didn't even pack. You don't even have clean clothes with you."

"Baby, I grabbed my spare suit and overnight bag from the office."

Sara still couldn't help but feel that this was all wrong; she didn't like this kind of last-minute surprise attack. "Well, this whole trip sounds rather unplanned. I don't like it," she confessed.

Finally, Sara heard the car engine come to a halt and the car door open. Nate replied, "Sweetie, I'll call you when I get to the ranch and give you all the details when I get back tomorrow."

There was another painful pause, so Nate filled it with "I love you, Mrs. Level."

"I'm sure you do, cowboy. What ranch?"

"Babe, I'll tell you tomorrow."

"Fine. I love you, too. Be careful out there. And call me as soon as you can."

With that, Sara heard the line click.

When Nate didn't call or answer his phone later that evening, Sara was pissed but not worried. Throughout their marriage, Nate had traveled extensively and he had gone incommunicado before, before cell phones. On more than one occasion his excuse was, "I fell asleep early." She interpreted that to mean a few too many at happy hour.

Sara sat next to the phone in silence, her mind wandering into the past, back to the time she first met Nate. She was only 23 and working a summer job for the construction firm Brown and Root. Nate was two years her senior and working on the same project as a contract administrator. Nate had just come off his tools, as it's called, as a high-rise ironworker. Once he completed his last night course for an undergraduate degree, the company had moved him into the corporate world, his first desk job.

Sara will never lose the picture in her mind of how he looked the first time she laid eyes on him. He was wearing a pearl button dark blue cowboy shirt, blue jeans, and black elephant skin boots. *What a butt*, she remembered.

Sara had plenty of opportunities as a young woman, but "This cowboy was different." He wasn't the typical guy she was used to dating. In his youth, Nate had a wild, adventurous side that ran miles deep, and Sara shared that trait as well. Two peas in a pod. Hard work, fast cars, good liquor, late parties, and honest friends. Sara would scream "Let the good times roll!" and hang her body out the window of the Mustang as they drove a 100 miles an hour down the country roads, both her hands in the air, margaritas in the cup holder. "Enjoy", as they put it, was their motto. They married within a year and their new motto soon became "Horses, Porsches, ranches, and fun."

Nate moved up the company ladder like a shooting star. They traveled the world from Saudi Arabia to Venezuela; California to Florida. After their first son was born, they were forced to reconsider their party plan. Nate went to law school, she had another baby, (another boy), and now after what seemed like mere seconds, they were empty nesters. Both of them eased the transition by seeing it as moving into their new beginning, their new era. Their life together was never boring and always evolving.

When Nate didn't call or come home as expected the next afternoon, Sara waited patiently for his lame excuse. But as darkness set in later during the night, she forgot about being mad at him. Sitting alone in the big house with only her thoughts, she began to worry. After a sleepless night, she started first light the next morning with a call to the office. After several attempts, she finally got through to Susy, who had confirmed Nate's travel arrangements and flight times.

"The phones and airlines out there aren't as reliable as in the States. I also understand it to be a rather large ranch. As big as the King Ranch here in Texas, so cell phones are spotty at best," Susy explained. Susy promised to call the client and get back to her immediately.

* * *

"Nate never came back from Ecuador," Susy said over the phone. "I've confirmed he made his flight to Costa Rica, but not the return."

There was a brief pause before Gordon spoke. "Let me call the client. Give me a minute and I'll call you right back," he said as he looked out the window of his safe house at the new Land Rover.

Gordon sipped his mimosa and waited 30 minutes. He fixed himself a fresh drink, then dialed Susy back.

Gordon took a deep breath before he began his one-act play.

"My God, Susy! It's awful! There was a plane crash. The jet went down over the Pacific less than 15 minutes after take-off. They were north of Ecuador, east of Columbia at thirty thousand feet. It's been confirmed. I was told no one could have survived. They can't even find the wreckage. A tower out of Bogotá got the Mayday and then lost the plane on radar. My God, Susy. Even if they find the wreckage, in all probability, they won't be able to recover any bodies. The authorities are nonexistent down there. You know how it is," Gordon spewed out the details at a fast pace and felt as though he had done well. He played her like a fiddle.

"Oh my Lord," Susy resounded. "Why weren't we informed sooner?"

Gordon let out a fake cry. "They were waiting for confirmation and maybe some good news. The search was called off this morning. They just don't have the resources to keep going. It's over. It's a fact now. Nate's gone."

"What do I tell Sara?" she blurted in shock.

Gordon acted upset. "Give me a minute to process all this. I'll call her. It's my responsibility. I should handle this. He was my partner after all."

"Oh, my word" were the only words Susy could muster.

*   *   *

Sara sat by the phone, waiting. She felt like she was going to be sick. Not only did she not know what else to do, but her mind was racing so fast she couldn't come up with a single coherent train of thought. Extreme scenarios bounced around in her brain. Was Nate hurt? Was he lost? Was there another woman involved? Had Nate finally had enough and was at this very moment sipping a piña colada in a Palapa bar somewhere in the tropics of South America with some dark-haired bimbo? Was he dead?

In the back of her mind, she always feared that he would leave her for a younger woman, but Nate would laugh it off when she'd tell him about it. He'd say her jealous streak kept him young and her in the gym. Sara knew these thoughts were only her insecurities, pure, unwarranted nightmares that came unwanted and ran like a freight train across her mind, out of her control. She rationalized that the answer lies somewhere in the middle of the fears. Her thoughts turned back to Nate and their life together.

Life without Nate was unimaginable. They both lived to please each other, which pleased themselves. Her life was Nate's and Nate's hers. She dressed in the fashion she knew Nate thought was sexy and worked out almost every day to keep her slim frame in line. They shared the same tastes for food, wine, and music and they had common goals. She lived her life for and with him first, the boys second, and she firmly believed the sacrifices she made throughout her life were great choices, no deep regrets. Her soul mate. She had lived a lifestyle beyond her wildest dreams and life without him was impossible to even imagine. But now Sara's mind was scrambled.

Her mind flashed to loved ones lost. Her deceased father had always said, "God, Family, Country." Sara would question him, asking, "Are you sure it's not Family, God, then Country?" Sara's life kept running through her mind like a wildfire burning out of control.

The phone rang. It was Gordon. She listened. She fell to the floor crying and everything went black.

Chapter 14

El Jefe

Santiago Valenzuela walked 400 yards through a dimly lit underground tunnel. He brushed off the sleeves of his lambskin jacket and surveyed the surroundings. He was standing in a dirt hole the size of a basement, with sunlight beaming down from an opening above a 2x4 ladder. A toothless, dark-skinned man holding an M1 carbine signaled him to climb up. Santiago squinted as he emerged into the sunlight. The toothless man followed, then ran over to the nearby Tahoe and opened the back door. Santiago straightened his jacket, rubbed the dust off his alligator boots on the back of his pant legs and climbed in. The dark tinted Tahoe kicked up dirt and sped away.

Santiago Valenzuela was born Juan Gomez-Gonzales in a whore house on the outskirts of Lazaro Cardenas, Mexico. His mother was dead by the time he was six and he quickly became a street urchin, forced to pack-up like dogs with the other orphans to stay alive. He killed his first victim at the age of eight. Juan and another child were sleeping in a dirt alley, behind a dumpster. The night was cold and they pressed together, trying to stay warm. Juan couldn't get warm and pressed tighter. His friend was asleep, wrapped in a blanket he had snatched off a clothesline. As Juan lay there shivering he saw a rusty pipe. He picked it up and got to his knees. He reared back with all his strength and landed a crushing blow to his sleeping friend's head. He hit him over and over as he watched the friend's head change to the color red as his brain matter soaked into the dirt. When his companion quit convulsing, Juan stole the blanket. He wrapped himself up in it, crossed his chest with the crucifix of Jesus, and laid against the dead corpse for warmth. Juan felt warmer and quickly fell asleep. The next morning he tossed the blanket on top of the dead boy and headed toward the port in hopes of finding some food. It was the first murder of many, and not as ruthless as most.

In the early years, Juan begged in the streets. He lowered his head, held out his hands and pathetically said "Por favor, por favor" following old ladies and gentlemen as they scurried down the crowded streets. When they turned away, he grabbed their wallet or purse and ran. He grew braver as he got older.

By the age of twelve, he made money doing odd jobs. He worked as a delivery boy for the drug dealers, a street hawker for the prostitutes, and a lookout for the thieves. Their trust took him off the angry streets and into the underworld. They taught him to cheat, steal, lie, and fight, and he was good at it. He learned to take what he needed, or wanted, by whatever means necessary. He found that murder was always a quick, easy solution. He practiced on strangers and learned the fastest, or slowest, way to make a human die. It never bothered him, he never felt a thing.

Juan once followed an unsuspecting couple as they turned onto an isolated side street. The woman was wearing a diamond ring and the man had on an expensive watch. He patiently watched as they opened the front door of their street-side apartment. He ran up behind the man and bashed the side of his head in with a rock. The man fell to the floor inside the apartment, paralyzed, but conscious. Juan found himself sexually aroused. He pushed the woman inside the doorway and closed the door. He forced the man to watch as he raped his wife, again and again. Two hours later he left with the watch, the ring, and thirty dollars.

By the time he was 18, he was hired out as an enforcer. Powerful, with plenty to prove, he demanded respect from everyone in his path. If it was not given to his satisfaction, a switchblade was the optimal solution. He changed his name when he earned the honor to finally take a seat at the big table. It was then he became known as Santiago Valenzuela, a proper name for respect, one befitting of his new station in life.

Santiago emerged as the head of a small but lucrative drug distribution network in his twenties, with a respectable revenue in the tens of millions annually. It was a grain of sand on the beach compared to cartel standards, but Rome wasn't built in a day. He was allowed to continue his solo operations by the grace of the large cartels, so long as the lion's share went to their coffers and Santiago played ball. Santiago's business flourished as his profits continued to grow. By his mid-thirties, he had systematically killed off the competition, expanded his business, and was now one of the largest, most feared kingpins in all of Mexico. Santiago had even larger ambitions and would stop at nothing to achieve them. His life seemed to be going places and he learned how to protect it.

Years ago, Santiago awoke one morning in a king size bed, surrounded by four naked women. He looked out the window and watched his horses gallop across the pasture on his fifty-acre compound. He loved it here. He relaxed and slapped one of the women on her naked ass. After he dressed in a purple warm-up suit, he walked to the veranda where the cook would serve him breakfast. He sat down at a wrought iron table and glanced back into the house through the floor-to-ceiling windows. Without any warning automatic gunfire broke the silence, shattering the windows, and pulverizing the furniture inside the house. Glass and debris flew everywhere. Santiago hit the ground and crawled for cover behind a stone column. He didn't have a weapon. He leaned around the column and saw three dead bodies and the cook pointing toward his bedroom. Four men in stocking masks ran toward the room. Santiago heard the screams over more automatic fire. He got off the ground and ran for the cover of the barn. More gunfire. Once inside he jumped on a four-wheeler, fired it up, and blew it out the open roll-up doors, full throttle, across the pasture.

After this, Santiago rarely slept in the same bed two nights in a row. He was forced to stay in constant motion. His success made him a prime target. They wanted his business. They wanted his money. They wanted his power. Over the years, caution aged into sociopathic paranoia.

One afternoon Santiago sat in a cabin watching the sunset over the Sierra Madres.

"Governor Díaz called," a bodyguard said.

"What'd he need?"

"He's throwing a party down in Puerto Vallarta. Wants to know if you can make it."

"What kind of party?"

"Black tie. Said it was a campaign shindig. If you go we can stay at Steve Rhyne's place on the mountainside. He's on his boat somewhere in the Caribbean. It's vacant."

"Good opportunity to change locales. We can do some tuna fishing, watch the whales and move on to Yalapa, smoke some of that hippy dope. Make the arrangements."

That was his life now. Santiago moved through towns, villages, and cities in the company of the affluent, staying in numerous safe houses that were luxurious, filled with the finest tequilas, the most expensive furnishings, and beautiful ladies. Santiago was a quick study and learned to enjoy the finer things in life as the money flowed. He had no illusions of how he got to where he was and how to keep it. He was ruthless and unforgiving.

"Kill'em all!" Santiago shouted.

He grabbed the naked man's hair, slammed his face into the counter and hit him again. The tortured man's face was purple, his eyes swollen shut, his body streaked in blood. His mother, his brother, his wife and his two kids were on their knees, bound and gagged, forced to watch in horror. Santiago took out a knife and dug a deep cross into the flesh of the man's chest. He then grabbed a pair of pliers and peeled the skin back.

"You steal my money!" Santiago spat in his face.

He then pulled out a pistol while another held the man's swollen eyes open. Santiago started with his mother and systematically shot every member of his family in the head. He turned, cut the man's balls off, and shoved them into his mouth. The man was still alive. He pleaded for mercy in Spanish. Santiago sat back, opened a beer, and watched. When he finished the beer he drove an ice pick in the man's eye that penetrated into the brain.

"That'll send a clear message." Santiago unzipped his pants and pissed all over the dead man.

Today Santiago wanted a different brand of revenge. He sat in the Chevy Tahoe as it traveled the 300 miles to Houston, and fumed at the dumb luck of the gringos that made this trip north of the border necessary. He pressed a cell to his ear.

"Is that you Blackie?"

"Si' jefe, estoy aqui."

"You make it to Houston without any trouble?"

"No problema. I flashed my green card. Sailed right through the checkpoint in Sarita. Got into town early this morning. You having any trouble with the border patrol?"

"No, no. Have you found Gordon yet?"

"No, jefe. If he's in town he's holed up somewhere we don't know about."

"Not likely, we've kept tabs on him for years. What about his partner's wife. The dead one."

"She's not around either. House is empty, one of the cars is gone. I think she's on the run."

"You think they're in this together?"

"No way. She way too good looking, and he's not that smart."

"You keep lookin' for 'em. Put the word on the street to find Gordon Manners and that mom. Let it be known that anyone who locates them will get a big reward."

"Already happening, jefe."

"Listen, Blackie. The bonds will surface, eventually. But I need the information on the flash drive now. You follow me?"

"I'm on it boss. I'll find it. Let me know when you get to town." Blackie waited for the call to disconnect, then dialed another number.

Santiago had eyes and ears everywhere. He had received a call telling him that the bonds were stolen thirty minutes after it happened. His network was efficient and operated on checks and balances. He was eating at Senor Frogs, in Mazatlan, at the time. He owned a piece of the touristy restaurant and a hotel on the beach. He went back to his penthouse, watched the Pacific Ocean roll its' waves onto the white sand beach and waited for more details.

"Who's responsible for this!" he hissed.

The condo safe was used to get important documents into the states, such as property deeds, contracts, and accounting records. Only his most skilled and trusted men had the combination. He knew the Cartel was merely window dressing in a more elaborate pyramid, controlled by unseen, silent forces. He called these players the shadow people. Santiago didn't know who they were but watched as they pulled strings like puppeteers. The bonds belonged to them. It was just another delivery to Santiago, to stay in their good graces and be allowed to move his drugs uninterrupted. All would be forgiven when the money was paid back. The information on the flash drive was different. That belonged to him.

"If the shadow people find out about the information, I'll disappear along with everyone who helped me get it," he said. The information would move him up the food chain through blackmail, bribery and their fear of it being made public. Santiago was learning that information was control and far more powerful than money, or his switchblade.

"What a joke," he said to himself.

"I know what it appears to be, but I know the real score. Those pendejos won't even meet. They wash my money with the stroke of a pen then use it to control countries and economies," Santiago reeled, wanting a seat at this adult table.

Now, seated in the back of the Tahoe, he looked at his Rolex and said, "When I find that Abogado and that widowed bitch, they'll beg to give me back my property. It'll take me less than a minute to get what I need from them. If this wasn't so important, I could have sent a local to do the job. I have to do this one personally. I can't have any screw-ups or excuses. And when I get what I came for, I'll get the hell out of this backward country."

Santiago rarely ventured into the Estados Unidos. It was dangerous. The federal government had him listed as the head of a dangerous drug cartel and he was on the FBI's most wanted list. He watched out the window as the flat, desolate South Texas landscape rolled by and dialed his phone. When a voice on the other end picked up, Santiago spoke.

"Gordon, you find that widowed bitch yet?" he asked, not believing for a second that Gordon didn't intend to perform his own disappearing act.

Chapter 15

The Funeral

Nate stood at the top of a small hill littered with oak trees, looking down at the reality of a dream he wished was different. He had imagined his own funeral would be attended by old friends from the past, judges who revered him, business associates, loved ones, distant family members, and admirers. Maybe even an old girlfriend or two hidden amongst the crowd. As he peered down the hill, all he saw gathering around his open grave and the empty casket was his wife Sara, his two boys, Uncle John, Gordon's secretary, and the preacher.

"I should have worked more on my people skills," he mumbled to himself. "Talk about a kick in the ego."

As he watched his casket being lowered into the ground, Nate admitted to himself that he was lucky he wasn't really in it.

Nate didn't remember everything that happened in Costa Rica, but he did remember the interrogation, the hot knife that pierced his flesh, the fall, and then laying at the foot of a cliff. The sheer agony of it all would best be forgotten, but he was positive this memory would not diminish over time.

The total pain he experienced in that moment was so clear to him that he could still taste the blood. He continued to relive that feeling of pain, over and over, time and time again. It came like a child screaming for his mother, afraid of the dark, and he knew it would for the rest of his life.

The next memory Nate recalled was waking up in a bed under a mosquito net. A young, dark-haired girl was sitting next to him. She looked like an angel. When he tried to sit up, he couldn't. He realized he was tied to the bed and terror once again flooded into him. He thrashed his arms and legs, scaring the young girl. She quickly yelled in what sounded like tongues, leaped from her chair and ran out of the room. As Nate tried to scream and struggle for his freedom, a thin, long-haired man appeared. The stranger was shirtless and tattooed, with two nipple piercings.

"Easy there, cowboy," the stranger spoke in a soft, soothing tone as he pulled the mosquito net aside and began to untie Nate's hands and feet. Nate stopped struggling.

"Had to restrain you to keep you from hurting yourself. You had some violent night terrors," the stranger spoke. "I was afraid you'd bite your own tongue off."

Nate's eyes focused intently on the stranger, identifying whether he was friend or foe with animal-like ferocity.

"Couple of kids found you buck naked at the bottom of the gorge with a knife hole in your belly. Broke a couple of ribs in the fall. Concussion. You were beat up pretty bad. If that knife went a few centimeters left, we'd be playin' taps rights now."

The stranger smiled as he calmly removed the restraints and continued, "Cuts, scrapes, bruises all over. Blood everywhere. You would have died for sure if those kids hadn't found you. Good thing we got to you when we did. Must be your guardian angel looking over your shoulder. All in all, good luck on top of what I'd imagine to be a pretty bad day, if I had to hazard a guess."

The man extended his hand. "You can call me Whip McCalister. That's W- H- I- P. Whip."

Nate slowly extended his injured arm, doing his best to ignore the lightning shooting through his nerves, and shook Whip's hand.

"Welcome to nowhere, " Whip said as he smiled.

Nate couldn't process this at all. When he realized he wasn't a prisoner, he calmed down as the events came swirling back in like a tornado. It was a tabletop puzzle, all in shades of blue; the questions were as confusing as the answers.

"Where am I?" Nate's labored words came in a raspy voice he didn't recognize.

"Town McCalister, I call it," Whip responded. "Been here fifteen years now." Whip handed Nate a glass of water and pushed a syringe into the IV in Nate's arm.

Nate sipped the water soothing his parched throat and managed to say, "What is this place?"

"Me and the wife came down here years ago to escape all the madness. Originally from the south of Houston. Got so crowded and crazy there I felt like a dog chasing his tail. In a nutshell, we came down here for a vacation, ended up backpacking the countryside and, well, stayed. Quit our jobs, took the wife's teacher pension, sold the house. Ended up growing dope for the Business. We don't call it the cartel down here, bad connotation and all. Not rocket science. Hell, not a secret either. Once they realized I could grow it and had a reliable distribution network to get rid of some of it on my own, they let me roll. I grow it, ship some of it for myself, give them their cut, and the locals' mule the bulk of it out. Fair size operation, if I do say so myself," he said, not looking up from the examination.

Nate wondered if Whip actually breathed in oxygen before starting the next sentence, "I started growing the superweed years ago before everyone else caught on. The Business thought I was like a genius chemist at first. They love the big money on such small quantities, comparatively speaking. A new niche for them at the time. I'm still putting my best buds in glass cigar containers, hermetically sealed, washed to kill the smell, and UPS them back to the States. The money is... well," he reared back lifting his eyebrows with a cocked smile. He shrugged his shoulders and went on.

"We built this town over the years, no dirt-floor huts here. You're in the hospital, only two beds, but the equipment and drugs are state of the art. The local nurse takes care of everything. I help with the patients if it's not too serious. This all works itself out. The locals have employment and a community. The Business provides a safe work environment. We're really just a small part of the bigger picture, a cog in the wheel as they say," Whip nonchalantly stated as he removed Nate's bandages, throwing them in the trash. Nate listened.

"Me and the wife are getting the Business into the legal stuff, you know, legitimate medical and recreational licenses. Now we got grow operations up in California, Colorado, Oregon, and Washington. Forget Alaska though. Too damn cold, too short a growing season. Stateside operations are booming. We'll soon be in Nevada, Arkansas, and Arizona. The newbie growers, our competition, if you want to call them that, are even buying our seeds like crazy. Used to throw them out with the stems. It's a win-win. The business down here is still in full swing and now we are selling it legal in the States. We're a regular Monsanto. What a country, eh Nate?" Whip put on his reading glasses as he finished removing the bandages, snickering.

Nate's head was spinning, and he was pretty sure it wasn't just from the concussion. "What about 'the dangers of drug running' and what not? The killers, Cartel drug lords, turf wars, blood in the streets and all that?" Nate asked.

Whip sat down on a swivel stool beside the hospital bed and looked Nate in the eyes. "They're around, but the people running the real Business, not the so-called drug lords, are businessmen. You know, politicians, bankers, doctors, lawyers, and such," Whip explained as he hummed a bar from that old Willie Nelson song, "Mamas Don't Let Your Babies Grow Up To Be Cowboys."

"All that depraved nonsense is for the Wild West wannabes. Those are 'cartel' smuck's trying to do it their own way. They are out of our fold entirely. They're considered rogue independents. They still have to share their profits with the Business, or they're put out of business. The people who run the Business are the real operators who do it on a much bigger scale than those boys you hear about in the news. They run partnerships with countries, governments, and any politician in power who needs a little extra dough for their re-election campaign. Loads of cash, like I said. A win-win for everyone."

Nate watched the old hippie as he doctored and asked, "You're not even a little afraid of the drug cartels?"

Whip shook his head back and forth, "no," wrinkling the corner of his mouth. "When the cartel cowboys get out of hand, the Business lets the United States taxpayers, bless their noble hearts, keep them in check. The bottom line is the US taxpayers keep our competition down for us and send us money like crazy. Good old Uncle Sam ships equipment, employment, and cold hard cash down here to support their make-believe drug war. A subsidy, if you will, and they keep the independent bad guys in check. So long as certain guidelines are followed by all participating parties, the Fed leaves us alone. You would think they were our partners. What a co-op for the Business, am I right, Nate? American market, American subsidized, American policed, and exempt from American antitrust laws and taxes. You know these guys make more money than Exxon. All cash. Go figure."

Whip paused, looking over his patient through his reading glasses and smiled again. "I don't do so bad myself." Nate wasn't sure if he was referring to his bank account or medical skills.

Is this guy for real? was all Nate could think. Or maybe he was just given an extra strong dose of something.

"How do you know all of this? Shouldn't this all be a secret?"

Whip grinned and shrugged his shoulders again like it didn't matter. "I have an undergraduate BBA in accounting from Baylor University, Masters of Business from the University of Texas, a Ph.D. in Finance from Yale, and I graduated from the school of corporate hard knocks and life on the short end of a chain a long time passed. Worked the whole time I was in school and paid for it myself. Bought the T-shirt and drank the corporate Kool-Aid until it made me sick. The American Dream it most certainly was not. This, on the other hand, is living, my friend. Like I said, no secret, not rocket science, not above your pay grade." Whip leaned over and whispered in Nate's ear, "They don't want to catch us, they already know," still grinning.

Whip concentrated as he smeared a salve on Nate's wounds. "Pretty ugly scabs. You have one ferocious guardian angel, I'll tell ya. You're healing like a pro. Could be the oxygen and antibiotics helped." Whip continued smearing more salve and, unsurprising to Nate, he went on…

"Not to get off the subject, but I ran a background check on you. You have been in and out of consciousness for three days now, had plenty of time. What do you say I get us some dinner and a couple of cold ones and I'll show you our landing strip? You'll like the corporate jet, I'm sure of it."

Whip sat back down on the stool, throwing the last of the bandages in the trash.

"I bet you're starving! Wander on down to the main house when you're ready and I'll have the wife rustle us up some dinner. Can't-miss it. It's the big hacienda at the end of the street. Clean clothes in the dresser," he said as he pointed across the room. With that, Whip made a shadowy exit, his long black hair bouncing down his back.

"Three days?" Nate stretched and sat up. He checked himself over. He saw stitches in his side, his bandaged chest, medicine on the table next to the bed and pink skin, head to toe. Nate removed the IV and sat on the side of the bed. He was stiff, sore, and his ribs hurt like hell, but otherwise, he felt like himself.

Whip's wife, Cindy, was social, happy, easy to look at and had a laugh that lit up the room. Whip and Cindy wined and dined Nate South American style, and eighteen hours later he was behind the wheel of a relatively new Four Runner at the Palacios airport in Texas, just two hours south of Houston.

"When you're through with the car just return it to any National Car Rental," the pilot told Nate. "Be sure to take Whip's advice to heart." Then he turned his attention to the attendant who showed up to refuel the jet at the airport. Whip made Nate's return to the U.S. unrealistically easy. His only advice was that any phone call or contact with anyone would be stupid and certain death for his family. No other helpful information was offered.

Who was that long-haired, over-educated, rich, pot-dealing gringo from the deep jungles of Costa Rica?

As Nate stood alone on the hill watching his own lonely funeral, he turned his mind to what he needed to figure out, what he would have to do, and how he was going to pull it off.

Chapter 16

First Contact

Sara raised her boys to be strong. She had devoted her life to them while also managing to stay fiercely in love with her husband. The boys took the death of their father as hard as any child would, but Sara soon realized that they viewed his death in a man's way: imminent. This was the life lesson their father had instilled in them. Die with your boots on.

The two boys stayed for only a night, at their mother's insistence. After their father's sunrise service, the short celebration of life was held back at the house. It was attended by only the boys and Uncle John. Afterward, they all flew home. The day was full of tears, hugs, kisses, memories, and assurances, but now they were off to their separate lives. Sara dropped the boys off at the airport and Uncle John grabbed an Uber. Her children promised to call.

Sara got back to the house from the airport and walked through the front door, alone. As she hung her purse on the hall tree the phone rang. She glanced around the room and saw it on the table behind the couch, instantly thinking it was left by one of the boys or Uncle John. She walked across the house and answered it.

"Hello?" she asked.

An electronically altered voice responded, "We know he's there, Sara. Save us the trip and put him on the phone."

Sara looked up startled. She stretched the phone forward with one hand and covered the mouthpiece with the other. "It's for you," her voice cracked.

Nate stepped out of the dark hall leading from the kitchen. He was eating the last piece of pecan pie the boys had so graciously left behind. He looked at Sara and started shaking his hands back and forth, signaling no.

*   *   *

Nate had called Sara from the first payphone he could find after leaving the Palacios airport. He was actually surprised how few were left in the world, or maybe it had just been fifteen-plus years since he needed one. He didn't care what anyone said, Sara needed to know what was happening and he needed her. She was always the smart one in the marriage after all, and he needed her wits now more than ever. Like any good relationship, they were in this together. They always had been, and always would be.

When Nate finally found a payphone, he went inside the Quick Stop and got a sack full of quarters from the attendant. He stood in front of a battered phone and pushed the change through the pay slot before dialing. Someone answered on the third ring.

"Hello," the voice said softly.

Nate hadn't thought it through and said the first thing that came to his mind, "Baby, it's me. I'm on my way home. You cannot tell anyone I'm alive. I'll tell you everything the second I get back. All the sordid details, I promise. I am about two hours out. But listen, babe, you cannot tell a soul. Not even the kids. I'm sorry."

He could hear Sara sob and shout incomprehensible words into the receiver, a reaction that was not at all surprising to Nate.

Nate continued, "Baby, I know this is a shock, but it's really me. I'm alive. Everything is going to be okay, I promise. Listen, I gotta go right now. I'll see you soon."

Before Nate could hang up the phone he heard his wife yell, "What the fuck is going on! Nate? Is that really you?"

*   *   *

Sara placed the phone back to her ear. "Nate passed away last week in South America. May I ask who's calling?"

The electronic voice firmly stated, "We know he's alive, Sara. We also know he's there with you right now, and we know about the trouble you've found yourself in."

The electronic voice went on, "We are forced into mutual interests. If you want our help, hand him the phone. Forgive the cliché, but you can do this the easy way or you can make things more difficult than they already are for you. You decide, Sara. He's right in front of you, hand him the phone and tell Nate to just listen."

With that, Sara exhaled and handed Nate the phone. Nate hesitated as he put the phone to his ear, his other hand dropping to his side, still holding the last bite of pecan pie. Nate just listened. After what seemed like an eternity, the phone went dead without Nate so much as saying a word. Nate looked at Sara and fell onto the couch.

Sara moved in front of Nate. "Who was that? What did he want?"

Nate could only say, "Instructions."

Sara's tone was confused. "Instructions? What kind of instructions?"

Nate looked up at Sara and asked, "Where did you get that phone?"

Sara shook her head. "It was just laying here. On the table. I thought one of the boys left it or maybe Uncle John. Nate, honey, tell me, what did he wanted. What instructions?"

Nate regained his composure as he nibbled more of that pecan pie. He stuffed the last bite into his mouth before speaking.

"You know, Sara, you make the best pecan pie."

"Nate!" Sara almost screamed. She waited for the details as she sat down at his feet, her face showing signs of anxiety, stress, and age.

Nate sighed. "He first asked me who I was going to trust. Then, what I think I was going to do. Although there was only one person on the phone, he kept referring to himself as 'we.' He explained my situation pretty accurately."

Nate focused on Sara, who sat attentive and unrelenting. "He started off by telling me what this looked like from the eyes of a law dog."

The voice said, "Come on, you're an attorney. Take a look at this. You entered the country without a passport under the cloak of darkness, you faked your own death, and now you're hiding from the authorities. You work for drug cartels in South America and have hidden money away for them in offshore accounts for years. It looks like you either stole money from the cartels or you're trying to escape the authorities with ill-gotten gains. How else can you explain your desperate attempt to disappear?"

Nate stopped to collect his thoughts and went on, "The voice was pragmatic. He listed all of the *exact* federal laws the government will say I am guilty of. Drug trafficking, organized criminal activity, tax evasion. He even thinks it's an easy RICO case against me. The voice told me that if I tell the truth, they'd laugh me right out of the courtroom all the way to prison. Said they wouldn't believe me and add a perjury charge on top of it all. But he always kept referring to himself as "we." He was like a spokesman for some group. He said I can beat the rap, but I can't beat the ride. I'll spend years and years fighting this in court, probably from behind bars, while all our assets are seized, frozen, or spent on my defense. I'm a rich parasite lawyer, after all. No one will believe me."

Nate looked down at Sara, still kneeling at his feet. "That electronic voice had an eerie tone. You heard it. It sent chills down my body. I've never heard anything like it. It didn't sound like any altered voice I've heard on TV. It was more refined, somehow crisper, clearer, cleaner. All I could do was listen. He explained, 'Go ahead, go to the police.' Which one? 'Houston Police Department, Department of Public Safety, Sheriff's Department, Federal Marshals, FBI, CIA. Take your pick.' And then he talked about the flip side, as he called it."

'Have you thought about Santiago?' the voice asked me. 'Do you remember the Mexican who thinks he killed you?' That's his name. He's missing money and he's coming to get it. He won't stop until he has it all back. This is fact, not fiction, Nate. Sara's not safe, your boys aren't safe and he just went on and on. He asked me how long I could play dead while my family's lives were in jeopardy."

Nate put his hands on Sara's shoulders and continued, "You know he's got a point. He made a little sense. He knew what I went through in Costa Rica. In that strange crisp tone, the voice informed me that this man is a cold, calloused killer. When he finds out I'm alive he'll finish what he started and then he'll wipe out our entire family. All of my seed from the face of this planet, just for laughs. 'It's the machismo thing,' the man said.

He then tried to rationalize with me. He, or she, or whoever that voice was, explained that I haven't thought this all the way through."

Sara listened quietly, wiping tears from her cheeks. It was a useless effort.

"He said, 'As a matter of fact, you don't know the score, Nate. Lay low while things blow over? Wait it out? See what happens? Bad plan, kiddo. All you could think of after your near death experience was getting home to your wife, eating some good ol' American food, and staying off the radar. It's doesn't work like that. You do know Santiago's men thought you were Gordon and when he found out different, he just killed you. Remember? Your partner sent you to your death. Your partner set you up.'

It was almost as if this man was concerned. He then went on to say, 'Here's the kicker, your saving grace. We need something that Gordon's got and you can get it for us. If you help us, we will protect you from Santiago."

Sara raised her head. "What did he say next?"

Nate finished, "He told me what he wanted."

Nate stopped, trying to recall what the voice said word for word. "He said, 'We can use you and Sara as our bait. We don't need to, but it could benefit both of us. You're in so deep, you have no clue and, quite frankly, no other option. Think about the players and the end result of all of this, Nate. You make the choice, but don't take too long.' After that, he gave me instructions and said, 'Follow them or not. If you do, we'll be in touch.' Then he hung up."

Sara dropped her head and asked, "What are we going to do?"

Nate reached down and pulled her head up. He looked her in the eye, took a deep breath, and answered, "We're going to do what he said."

Sara frowned as she looked back into Nate's eyes. "What did he say to do?"

Nate jumped to his feet, "Road trip! Pack your bags, baby! We're headed for the casinos in Biloxi, Mississippi!"

Sara squinted, "Are you serious?"

"Let's roll!" Nate blurted out as he did a train shuffle toward the stairs.

"Who do we trust?"

"Only each other. As always."

Chapter 17

Another Day at the Office

Detective O'Hare and his wife knelt at the altar in St. Mary's Episcopal Church as they prayed and prepared to receive Holy Communion, or The Lord's Supper as it was so called in his youth. O'Hare's wife was a deeply devout woman and had been her entire life. She sat this Wednesday morning, as she did at least once a month, at the table of Jesus participating in the sacrament of Eucharist to avow the bonds with other Christians and her redemption by the Blood of the Lamb. O'Hare's wife, Elise, insisted her husband join her at church. A Catholic by birth, O'Hare found this time with his wife, along with the peace of the church, to be a welcome part of their life and a welcome change from the blood, guts, and pure evil that was ever present in his daily routine. He knew himself to be a stone cold sinner compared to his wife, but he'd possibly be up for sainthood when compared to some of his collars. The severity of sins was not his strong suit.

O'Hare looked up from prayer and gazed over at his wife as she received the symbolic body and blood of Christ. She was hanging onto the chalice containing the blood of Jesus with both hands as if her soul depended on it. After giving her a sip, Father Mark wanted the chalice back in order to move on with Communion. However, Elise would have no part of it. She was pulling the chalice back toward her lips, leaning forward over the prayer rail for what looked like another shot of the wine. They used real wine for communion, not that fake stuff. Elise kept tugging the chalice her way, while Father Mark continued tugging the chalice his way. Neither was willing to surrender and there was a stalemate at the Lord's Table, during the Lord's Supper, over the blood of our Lord Jesus.

All O'Hare could think of was, *Holy shit, Batman!*

He reached over and gently touched his wife on the thigh.

Elise cut her eyes at him and whispered out of the corner of her mouth, "I didn't get a sip."

"It's okay. Let go."

"No," Elise grimaced as she pulled harder, causing Father Mark to rearrange his stance, getting better leverage. The tug of war was game on.

"Elise, let go," O'Hare said again.

"He didn't give me any," she proclaimed as she now glared at Father Mark as if trying to will him through telekinesis to cooperate as if her life depended on it.

O'Hare once again reached over, only this time poking Elise on the thigh with his finger. Elise responded by letting go of the chalice. Father Mark fell back a full step, almost spilling the wine, but caught himself on his back foot. Father Mark rearranged his robe, gained his composure, and moved on to the next parishioner. He shot the evil eye at Elise.

As the two regained their seat in the church pews, O'Hare's phone vibrated. It was the precinct. He showed his wife. She nodded and shook her head that she understood. It was commonplace in their lives. O'Hare gave her a kiss on the cheek, exited the pew crossing his heart with the sign of the cross, and walked out to his car.

Perfect timing, he thought. "Hey Gini, what's up?"

"We got the ballistics back," Gini said.

O'Hare was puzzled. "All five slugs, the pistol, and the shotgun? Unheard of this fast. Must be a slow week at the crime lab." O'Hare smiled. "Well, don't keep me in suspense. What's the verdict?"

Gini toyed, "Go ahead and guess."

O'Hare was up for it. "The 10 mil from Galveston matches both rounds fired at the attorney's condo that killed the Latino. The 9mm slugs from the wall and security guard are untraceable and the shotgun is a smooth bore so ballistics can't help. How close am I?" he responded as he played with the newbie.

Gini's thunder was stolen. Her tone was as if someone had discovered a deep dark secret that only she was supposed to know when she said, "Looks like you get a gold star, detective. How did you know?"

O'Hare unlocked his car. "It's why they call me a detective, Gini. What do we have on the headless guy and dozed Plymouth?"

Gini went over the headless man's history, now known as Jack Middlebrooks. She ran through the highlights with O'Hare on the phone. A high school dropout, a short stint in the Marines, Special Forces in Vietnam. Rode with an outlaw motorcycle gang in the early '70s. Worked odd jobs, no serious criminal history, and no known friends or family. Lived in a trailer in San Leon, Texas. Pretty much a dead end.

O'Hare was not surprised and reassured Gini, "I'm on my way to the office. Keep digging. Check out Gordon's law firm too, will ya'? We'll go over what you got when I get there."

O'Hare scratched the back of his neck, thinking, *This case was too clean. It made no sense but was coming together fast and easy. What was in the safe? Follow the bodies.* He then chuckled as he remembered watching his wife wrestle with Father Mark over the chalice of wine.

Chapter 18

Nutria for Lunch

Nate and Sara loaded two small suitcases into the rear of their Yukon and a small cooler in the back seat. Before Nate hunkered down in the floorboard of the front passenger side of the car to remain unseen, he turned to Sara and confirmed, "No I.D., no credit cards, no cell phones. Nothing that can be traced back to us, right?"

Sara nodded and said, "Not even a monogrammed shirt. I have three thousand dollars in cash from the safe and with the exception of this car, we're totally incognito. You know that amount of money won't last us long."

Nate crouched his large frame onto the floorboard, saying, "Something tells me we are dealing with professionals. We'll follow their instructions as long as it works for us."

Sara hit the button for the automatic garage door opener and backed out. She thought out loud, "Nutria? With a side of venison boudin? Yuck." Sara stuck her tongue out. "That's gross."

As Nate tried to stay hidden he responded, "That's what he said. Those were the instructions. Order it at a place called Seafood B Bobb's outside of Lake Charles, Louisiana."

Nate went on. "The instructions are to ask for Bryan Bobb and tell him it's to go. Order a nutria basket with onion rings, 1-½ links of venison boudin, and if he asks any questions it's alright, just answer them and ask how long the alligator will take to cook."

Sara knew this was beyond weird and asked, "Nate, is this actually for real? Are you sure?"

Nate responded, "Give us a better option, Sara. That electronic voice or whoever the 'we' were on the phone knew I was alive. If they know it, who else does? Our original hide-and-see plan's a wash. The least we can do is play this one out and see where it goes."

Once they were away from the house, Nate got up from the floor-board as he and Sara headed for Biloxi, Mississippi, via a nutria basket for lunch in Lake Charles, Louisiana.

The trip from Houston to the east of Lake Charles took less than two and a half hours. Seafood B Bobb's turned out to be a hole-in-the-wall made of old wood planks and rusted tin. When the two opened the front screen door, it squeaked so loud it startled Nate. Once inside, the definite odor of fried food was unmistakable, but what kind of fried food was a mystery smell. Although it was three in the afternoon, which was too late for the lunch crowd and too early for supper, the place was packed. The two waited in line and once they got to the counter, as instructed, they asked for Bryan Bobb and told the lady taking the orders, "It's to-go." In some kind of Martian language, they were told they were in the wrong line. Her accent was strong Louisiana Cajun. Had she not pointed and shook her finger, then whistled and redirected their eyes to where she was pointing they would not have seen the sign that said, "To-Go Orders Only." They moved out of that line and stood beneath the sign. A man about 5 foot 6 inches tall, built like a mountain and wearing a white apron that had never seen soap, appeared from behind the counter to take their order. In a raspy voice that had been hardened by a lifetime of smoking and straight whiskey, the man said with a thick Texas twang, "I'm B Bobb. What'll it be?"

They placed their order.

"Where y'all comin' from?" B Bobb asked with a Texas drawl as he wrote down the order.

Sara answered with her bright Texas smile, "Houston. How long will it take to cook the alligator?"

B Bobb didn't look up from the order pad. "Where y'all going?"

Sara smiled again. "Biloxi."

"Long way from Houston. Need a good car ta make sure ya don't get no trouble. Bad gettin' stranded out there in the delta. What ya driving?"

Bryan Bobb was covered in tattoos, bald, and had a ratty goatee, but despite his appearance, he came across with a genuine friendly demeanor. He struck a chord with Sara and, since small talk was her forte, she engaged the conversation.

"We're driving a brand new Yukon."

This time B Bobb looked up, smiled back, and told them, "Ya know we don't serve no nutria rat. Tried it. Made people all queasy, thinking we all's cutting up beaver rat next to the regular food. Ain't deer season neither. Sorry 'bout that. Alligator take, say, 'round 20 minutes. Worth the wait. Fresh as an old man. I'll put ya down for two to go, little lady. You and the big guy have a seat and we'll get ya some banana pudding, on the house, whiles ya wait. Sweet tea or plain, ma'am?"

Sara enjoyed the sound of home. B Bobb's accent and hospitality reminded her of where she grew up. She couldn't help but beam. She shrugged in agreement saying, "Regular for me, sweet tea for the big guy."

Bryan Bobb gave her the feeling of security that she lived in during her teens. Sarah giggled.

When the bell on the counter rang that their order was up, Nate and Sara refilled their tea glasses, grabbed the to-go bag, and headed for the car.

As the two walked to the car, Nate blurted out, "Man, that banana pudding was good! What was all that southern charm, eye batting about anyway? "

Sara didn't respond. She knew Nate felt the hometown feeling.

"Do you remember where we parked?" Nate asked, puzzled.

"Somewhere over there," Sara pointed. The place was still packed and the parking lot was full.

Nate hit the panic button on the remote. "There it is," he announced as the horn and lights gave up the location.

When Nate slid behind the steering wheel, he had a strange feeling and knew something was different. He wasn't sure what it was, but something had changed. He started the car, deciding it was only his paranoia. He told himself he needed to stay sharp and paranoid was good. Sara was getting the food ready to eat, laying it out on the center console and before Nate put the car in reverse, she put her hand on his arm, touching him to stop. She reached over and handed him a plastic sack from inside the order bag. Sara's face went pale. Nate opened the bag and found two Mississippi driver's licenses, one for each of them, two credit cards, one in his name and one in Sara's, and there were two well-worn wallets, complete with pictures, auto insurance card, health insurance card, and an AARP card. The names were the same except the last name was spelled Leval instead of Level; address 1234 1st Street, Biloxi, Mississippi 39533. Easy enough to remember, even under pressure. There was also another cell phone.

Nate studied the car again and realized it wasn't his paranoia. The car was different. He got out and looked at the front and then the back. The car had Mississippi plates and the Texas inspection and registration sticker on the window had been replaced by a Mississippi window sticker. He wasn't positive, but the VIN plate under the windshield might have been replaced as well. This was clearly a wakeup call and both Nate and Sara woke up. The situation was far more serious than they imagined. Who would go to all this trouble? Who were these people? What had he gotten Sara and himself into? What did the electronic voice want? What mutual interest? Nate's heart dropped when he remembered what the voice on the phone said: he was the bait.

Sara took a bite of their to-go meal.

"This alligator is delicious," she proclaimed. "They're like chicken fingers, but sooooo much better. Try a bite. The gravy's out of this world. No wonder that place was packed. Look at these onion rings!"

"We need gas," Nate said as he popped an onion ring in his mouth. "Let's see if these credit cards are any good."

He grinned, "Damn that is good. Hand me a piece of that alligator," and with that, the two headed toward Biloxi, Mississippi, without knowing why.

Chapter 19

Biloxi

The instructions given to Nate and Sara were plain enough. They didn't understand the reasoning behind it all and they felt like two children minding their parents for fear of a spanking. The real fear, though, was whether they were following the instructions to their death. Dead because of a wrong decision made by a total stranger that they didn't know and never met. Fate or even blind luck could not be so cruel or mysterious. Nate and Sara agreed that this was their best plan for now, or at least until they could come up with a better one.

The two checked into the Golden Nugget Hotel and Casino in Biloxi as instructed. A tropical storm had entered the Gulf of Mexico and the weather was taking a nasty turn. The winds were picking up, the bay was turning to chop, and to Nate, it just smelled like rain. Reservations had been made in their new aliases and when they flashed the new credit card to check in, it worked again. They were being played like pawns in a five-cent dime store novel.

Nate threw their two small bags on the bed in the hotel room and parked the little rolling cooler in the corner.

"Nice room," he said.

Sara walked to the window, opened the curtains, and looked out at the day slowly coming to a close. Nate followed and stood beside her. The room overlooked the golf course and pool. The pool was called "The H2O" and looked like the perfect place to unwind and feel the stress melt away. Lounge chairs built for two surrounded the edge of the pool and were strategically placed in the middle, framed by the crystal blue water. A bar ran the entire length on one side. It looked relaxing, something they needed after the last few days. They stood motionless in front of the window, with Nate's arm around Sara, and Sara's head on Nate's shoulder.

"I need a drink. No. Two."

Sara chimed in, "You mean three."

"Get the key and let's go," Nate said as he headed for the door, Sara moving with him in sync.

Both wanted to decompress and a few drinks at the pool bar might do the trick. Maybe play the slots and get a freebie. As they walked out of the hotel room, they were suddenly slammed back into their darkness. The cell phone rang. They both stopped dead in their tracks as Sara pulled the new phone from her purse. They both looked at it with blank stares.

"This is getting waaay spooky," Sara said. Suddenly the pressure was too much and she broke into a tirade.

"Nate, we didn't do anything. We didn't deal drugs, we didn't launder money, we haven't hurt anyone. We worked hard all our life, sacrificed, and raised two wonderful boys. Now, in what is supposed to be the easy part of our lives, we're hunted by a crazed drug lord who thinks he ended your life because of what turns out to be a sleaze bag, lying, double-dealing, no morals, shithead lawyer who was your partner! Nate, on a business trip, some Mexicans think they murdered you! You were found dying by a long-haired dope grower who saved your life, then sent you home on a freakin' Lear jet. You told me to bury you. You said you needed to stay dead. Your sons think you're dead! You said if we lay low, this will all sort itself out. We decided as long as they thought you were dead, we wouldn't be in any danger. Boy, did we get that one wrong. Now we're following instructions from a burner phone given by an unknown electronic voice."

Sara rambled on as the phone continued to ring. "We're using fake names and what the hell are we doing in, of all places, a casino in Biloxi? Now a phone that showed up in a to-go sack rings and I'm too fucking scared to answer it! I'm really scared, Nate. I don't care if it is a new iPhone. I am just flat scared to death! Electronic scary voice man has good taste in phones, but he also had the plates and registration changed on our car while a bald, tattooed short order cook fried us alligator. Nate, what is going on? Seriously, we're in too deep. Where will these instructions take us? We're out there in some sort of creepy secret agent spy land! On the drive out here we decided to play this smart. We need to think this through again."

All Nate could think to say was, "The phone's still ringing. You should answer it."

Sara picked up the phone, swiped the call icon, and answered, "H-h-halloo" in the sweetest southern accent she owned.

"Sara, this is Gordon."

Sara sat down on the side of the bed, silently mouthing Gordon's name to Nate. Nate's eyes went wide open and he leaned his ear into the phone.

"Sara, we need to meet. Where are you?" Gordon asked.

Sara spoke plainly, "Gordon? I haven't heard from you since before Nate's funeral."

"This is important, Sara. I'm afraid I have discovered some facts about Nate's death that you need to hear in person. Where are you?"

Sara continued, remembering the instructions, "I'm not in town. I had to get away. I'm visiting an old friend in Montgomery. I don't know when I will be back."

* * *

Gordon had this conversation all laid out like a script and proceeded with scene one. He knew at once he had no chance of finding Sara in Alabama. He had never had a personal conversation with Sara and in no uncertain terms did not know any of her friends, especially old ones. Her life was a mystery to him, and Nate's too for that matter. Outside of what he could get them to do for him or what he could selfishly talk them into doing, he didn't know too much about either one of them.

Gordon had to meet with her to lay the groundwork. He would tell Sara just enough to plant a seed of doubt about Nate and keep himself in the clear with Santiago. He would give her enough false information so that when she was interrogated by Santiago, the information would make Nate look like the culprit. It was his best shot, as long as he stayed cool and in control. Gordon moved forward with the plan.

"Sara, what I've learned is, quite frankly, a shocker. I can hardly believe it myself."

Sara acted surprised and, as instructed, asked, "Well, what is it?"

Gordon responded, "You have to hear this firsthand, in person."

He paused, then went on, "Were you and Nate having trouble? Was there another woman in Nate's life?" Gordon played the jealous card.

Sara responded quickly. "What! Gordon, what are you talking about?"

"Sara, listen. This won't wait. Let me think. Let's meet in Biloxi. That's about halfway for both of us."

Gordon mouthed *Touchdown* and pumped his fist. He could stay where he already was and get Sara to come to him.

He was confident, continuing, "I can make the drive first thing in the morning. It's about a six and a half hour drive for me from Houston and about four hours for you from Montgomery. How about we meet at two o'clock tomorrow at the Hard Rock Casino."

"Casinos are not friendly places, Gordon. I always feel uncomfortable in them. If you say this is urgent, I believe you. If I need to come, I will," Sara replied, following the instructions to a tee.

"Let's say seven o'clock at Beauvoir, the Jefferson Davis home in Biloxi. We can meet in his cottage. You know where that is, Gordon?" Sara set him up. The shoe was on the other foot. The hunter was now the hunted.

Gordon was thinking *"Gotcha,"* but instead said, "See you there at seven."

*   *   *

Sara hung up the phone and looked at Nate. Both were wondering how the voice knew Gordon would call, how they knew Gordon would want to meet in Biloxi, and how Gordon got the number to this phone that neither one of them knew.

Nate took a breath and said, "I think I need that drink now."

Sara replied, "What do you say we get a bottle of something and bring it back to the room?"

"I'd say that's a great idea."

Nate questioned, "You want pizza, chicken, or Chinese?"

Sara replied with a faint smile, "It's not our credit card, let's do room service."

Chapter 20

Santiago

Santiago Valenzuela had a string of safe houses from northern Mexico to Peru. He moved freely throughout Central America; Mexico, Guatemala, Belize, Honduras, El Salvador, Honduras, Nicaragua, Costa Rica, and Panama. He chartered planes with clandestine pilots and flew throughout South America as well. He spent time in Columbia, Brazil, Peru, Venezuela and had unlimited access to a ranch in Ecuador. He paid off the police, governors, bankers, politicians and just about everyone who was anybody. And it worked. The people who didn't really know him loved his charity. Soccer balls, goal nets, and church donations kept the impoverished on his side. The people who did know him were afraid of him.

In Houston, there wasn't a network of safe havens. Santiago had to be extra cautious and well protected. Although his reputation was well known by everyone tangled up in his business, north of the border his connections were only street level, not the power brokers he was accustomed to.

Once he arrived in Houston he drove to the second ward, better known as "the Barrio". For years his operation sent drugs here for distribution.

This part of Houston is controlled by the Tango Blast, the most notorious Mexican gang in the U.S. They are virtually unknown to law-abiding citizens, but not to anyone moving in the undercurrents of society. With 19,000 members located in all major U.S. cities, they were a major distribution network. One of Santiago's networks.

The Tahoe pulled up in front of a three-bedroom clapboard house. The paint was peeling and the screen on the front door was torn. The light showed through the bed sheets that were tacked up in the windows. A row house for the working poor, post World War II. The front yard was all dirt, surrounded by a rusted chain link fence.

"Is this the best you can do?" Santiago asked.

The driver responded, "It's only for tonight. Diego's meeting us here. We'll move in the morning."

"What a shit hole. Reminds me of that night in Boca del Torres."

One of his bodyguards smiled, showing his gold front teeth.

Two of the bodyguards exited the vehicle to check the house. One stayed behind. A minute later they signaled the all clear from the front porch. Santiago walked in the front door and was greeted by Diego, a commander in the Tango Blast.

"What an honor, jefe. Hope this'll do for tonight. This is the heart of our territory, it's safe. The law won't come near this block."

Santiago surveyed the room. There were two guys lounged on a ratty couch and one sitting in a filthy wingback. On top of the coffee table was a tray of dope. Beer bottles littered the room and a mirror with powder on it lay next to the chair. All three guys wore sleeveless undershirts and were covered in tattoos. Diego wore a long sleeve shirt and blue jeans. He was the only presentable one in the bunch and the only one who stood up when Santiago entered the house.

Without warning, Santiago pulled a handgun from his shoulder holster and fired two rounds. One hit each man sitting on the couch in the middle of the chest. At the same time, his bodyguard produced a rope and wrapped it around the throat of the man in the wingback. Another guard kept Diego from moving by holding a gun to his head. Santiago walked over to the man gasping in the chair.

"Do you know what respect is?" Santiago hissed.

The choking man couldn't speak. He struggled and grabbed at the rope. The third guard stepped forward and landed a hard blow in the middle of the gasping man's chest, then held his hands down on the chair.

"Here's a lesson you can teach your children," Santiago said.

He reached into his pocket and pulled out a knife. With a flip of his wrist, it clicked open. He placed it on the man's little finger, put the palm of his hand on the back of the knife, and pressed down with all his weight. The severed finger landed on the floor, blood soaking into the fabric of the chair.

Santiago nodded to the guard tightening the rope and he loosened his grip, allowing the man breath. The man in the chair let out a gut retching scream. No one worried about the noise. The sound of gunfire and screams were more common in this neighborhood than street lamps.

"Those were two of my best lieutenants," said Diego, unfazed.

"Nobody… that I don't tell myself… gets' to know I'm here. If someone else does, I'll kill them too. I'm takin' no chances," Santiago answered.

Diego was calm and pointed to the chair, "What about that one?"

"Haven't decided. Le' me ask him a few questions and I'll make up my mind."

The gun in Diego's face was lowered. He was on a first name basis with violence, but he didn't have a name to call this. The turmoil happened in seconds and was over as fast as it started. Santiago picked up the mirror and blew off the powder. He replaced it with a fresh pile and lowered his head. After snorting up the snow in one nostril, then the other, he leaned back and shook his head. He wiped the white stuff off his face and turned to the guards holding the man down.

"Get the duct tape out of the car and tie this bag up. I got some questions. I need to see if the answers please me."

He turned to Diego, "If they don't, your next. No one you ever meet is as tough as they think. Let's see who else knows I'm in town. If I don't like the answers, I'll send for your wife and girlfriend. I'll see what they have to say. Then me and the boys will have some fun. You can watch."

Chapter 21

New Suspect

Detective O'Hare hung up the phone with the Ecuadorian embassy. This case had now taken on a new twist. The call was supposed to be a simple follow through, part of the mundane, tedious, day-to-day bump and grind that O'Hare did for all his cases. Routine police work that rarely produces leads or valuable information. Only this call actually did. He put both elbows on his desk and rubbed his forehead. O'Hare always went through the motions and followed standard procedure to eliminate any possible suspects, however remote. The maids, tenants, and the personnel at the condo had all checked out and were systematically crossed off his suspect list. O'Hare was wading through Gordon Manner's family, friends, girlfriends, associates, partners, and employees as well. Other than his employees, it was a very short list,

O'Hare dreaded this part of the job. It was boring and kept him tied to his desk, but the suspect list grew shorter the longer he worked. Gordon's partner, Nate Level, seemed an unlikely suspect at first, but routine dictated that he check him out anyway. He had called the embassy to verify the plane crash and eliminate Gordon's partner as a suspect.

O'Hare first checked Nate out on a computer, using one finger to type his full name into the search engine. He stared at the results.

"What? This guy's dead? Bullshit," he said.

"Who's dead and why is it B.S.?" Gini asked.

O'Hare shook his finger saying "I'm working over here, try and keep it down will ya."

"W-h-a-t--E-v-e-r," Gini came back.

If it hadn't been for the obituary, he might have missed it. After a little detective work, O'Hare learned the guy died in some make-believe plane crash the day after the robbery. Because the story was so bogus and easy to verify, O'Hare couldn't make sense of it. Surely this legal eagle wasn't that stupid. The computer had spilled the facts about Nate's life in an instant. He had waded through that information, made the call to the embassy, and now had to add him to the list.

O'Hare leaned back in his chair going over the probable motives for this new suspect. He grimaced as he walked himself through each one.

Nate had been married for some thirty odd years. There could be another woman involved, always a reliable motive for murder. But this didn't pass muster.

Nate practiced law for twenty-five years, so he knew the ins and outs of law enforcement. O'Hare was sure he'd be smart enough to realize how easy it was to fact-check a plane crash. Dead end.

His kids were grown, successful in their own right. His wife was a stay-at-home mom. Nothing special there. He slapped the palms of his hands on the desk with a thud.

"Nate fits into this puzzle somehow, but I don't see any quick link, no smoking gun," he said out loud.

O'Hare shook his head, leaned forward in his chair and said, "Why would a guy fake his own death? What's he running from, who's he running from, what's he trying to hide?"

Despite the obvious, O'Hare couldn't bring himself to the conclusion that Nate fit as a suspect in a double murder and robbery. It didn't add up. His instincts told him better, but he left Nate on the suspect list anyway.

"You never know in this line of work," he said, drumming his fingers on the desk.

After hours of hard work, the list boiled down to something very short. The suspect list included Gordon Manners, the headless man now known as Jack Middlebrooks, and the newly resurrected Nate Level. He might come up with another suspect in this case, but somehow he doubted it.

Detective Gini Gibbs walked up and put the vanilla milkshake O'Hare had ordered for lunch on his desk. She explained matter-of-factly, "You know that ice cream and milk is nothing but cow fat and sugar. It'll kill you. Bad for the heart, cholesterol, liver, and packs on the pounds like blowing up a balloon. You should eat more sensibly."

"Funny, you don't look like my wife," he retorted as he sipped his milkshake.

Gini sat down at her desk next to O'Hare, eating her bran muffin, and spoke, "What do you think of this Nate fellow? Think we got our man?"

"No," O'Hare spoke, "You call his wife?"

Gini answered, "Yeah, no answer. Sent a cruiser to the house. No one home. Looks like a conspiracy to me."

"What else you got?"

Gini attempted to look sharp, sat up straight, and in her authoritative voice said, "All the usual suspects have been eliminated. All the staff at the condo checked out. All of his employees checked out. Manners doesn't seem to have any friends or a steady girl. No insurance fraud, no claims were filed. Dead end on the dead Mex at the condo… go figure. The dead security guard was involved somehow, can't get any answers out of him. Checked him out and his only life was to close down that dive bar off of Main Street. His drinking buddies at the bar weren't surprised a bit, to say the least. Bunch of drunk losers."

O'Hare slurped his milkshake. "Did you go over the physical evidence again?"

Gini bit her lip, "The three 9mm pistol slugs, the two in the wall at the condo and the one in the dead guard, all came from the same gun. Probably fired by the dead Hispanic at the condo. There was gunpowder residue on his hands and his fingerprints were all over the safe. But the prints and the ballistics don't match anything in our system. No I.D. on that dead man."

She paused for effect and went on,

"We've recovered the 10 mil that shot him and a shotgun from the wreck in Galveston. Neither gun was registered, of course. Partial print on the shotgun, but that's another dead end as well, the print was too damaged."

"The headless guy in Galveston was shot in the thigh with a shotgun, probably the one with the partial print. My theory is he was bleeding out when he decapitated himself. That was gross by the way."

"Having fun yet?" O'Hare asked.

Gini rolled her eyes. "Based on the scene at the car wreck, it appears our headless guy was chasing someone or being chased. We also couldn't get a traceable tire print on the other vehicle. They were all going sideways. Must have been a hell of a chase."

Gini paused and gathered her thoughts. "No stolen property reported at the murder scene either."

O'Hare finished the rest of his breakfast milkshake and after letting out a loud slurping sound asked, "What else do we know?"

Gini stopped and looked for approval, or really any reaction from O'Hare at all, and went on.

"No forced entry. A multi-million dollar piece of paper was still hanging on the wall after the break-in, a Picasso no less. Gordon Manners seems like an unlikely suspect because he claims there wasn't anything of value in the safe, and we verified he was in Vegas at the time of the break-in. This Nate Level isn't dead, but there was a funeral and his soon-to-be ex-widow won't answer the phone or return our calls. Then there's our headless man who was chasing someone or being chased, but no witnesses. He had a murder weapon on him." Gini sighed. "That's about all I got."

O'Hare shook his head. "Not even close grasshopper."

"How do you see it?"

"Let me lay it out for you," O'Hare explained. "Two people came in the back entrance after the night security opened the door for them. The door was jimmied but the jam wasn't completely broken, a sloppy mistake. It was raining that night. You missed the water spots on the floor by the back door and stairs. You could tell it was two people from how the water pooled by the door and the wet smudges running up the stairs. We now have two people and the security guard involved."

O'Hare took a deep breath. "The key was still in the door. It was brand new and had no wear and tear. It was either stolen then copied, or copied and given to them. The three entered the condo and caught the man inside off guard. The guy they found inside already had the safe open. The safe wasn't cracked, his prints were in all the right spots. He was surprised all right. He saw the uniform on the security guard and killed him, then shot a couple of rounds at whoever was left standing."

O'Hare talked slower, "It was probably that Jack guy who shot him, we have the gun he fired after he was opened up on first. He put the second round in him on impulse. I can sum the rest up by saying the two perps left standing grabbed the money and ran. Cops were there in less than five minutes after the 911 calls."

"So the only thing you don't know is their sex," Gini quirked.

O'Hare never looked up at Gini and continued. "There is a double cross somewhere in this fiasco. Jack was shot and died trying to chase somebody or something down, probably to get payback or his share. We still have at least one person with the stolen goods. I'm guessing that whatever it is, it's worth a fair bit of money."

"People don't go around shooting at each other and dyin' for nothin'. When you got three dead guys, there's money involved. Nothing stolen? I wouldn't bet on it."

"Now there's a new wrinkle, Nate Level. Like you say, we got three suspects. One's dead. One who doesn't give a tinker's damn about nothin' or no one. And one we can't find. My gut tells me Gordon Manners is wrapped up in all this. He's too cool, acts like it's no big deal, doesn't ask any questions, maybe because he already knows the answers to 'em. Nate Level, though, is the new fly in the ointment. He flies to San Jose the morning of the murders and no flight records of him coming back? His wife buries him? Now we can't find them? Call me crazy but murder doesn't fit him no matter how you slice it, it doesn't fit his modus operandi. And as far as the headless guy goes, he doesn't really matter anymore, now does he?"

O'Hare reached for his keys, still talking. "Nate's the guy we need to get answers from. Fat chance finding him, though. But we find his wife, and we find Nate. That's where we go to unravel this case."

Gini was puzzled. "So you got this all figured out, eh? For the record, no one told me about the key still being in the door or the water by the backdoor."

O'Hare answered her as he walked away pointing at the phone, "You missed it by looking at all the blood and guts. Find Sara."

"Where you going?" Gina yelled as O'Hare headed toward the elevators.

"See a judge about a horse," O'Hare said over his shoulder.

Gini looked mistreated and whined, "How come you get to have all the fun?"

"Seniority, my dear Watson," O'Hare said without looking back. "I'll call you if I can get the warrant and we can go see how the rich folk live."

Chapter 22

The Black Mosquito

No one knew, or cared, how he got his name. The Black Mosquito just fit him, so everyone called him Blackie for short. His roots lie in the ancient civilization of the Incan Empire dating back to 3,200 B.C. It had been the largest empire in pre-Columbian America and was conquered by the Spanish in the 16th century. He was small, stealthy, and a master at deception, but the value he brought to the table was his connections. His father, long dead, was a migrant farm worker. Blackie grew up picking crops from California to New Jersey, Florida to Texas. He knew the backdoors, the black markets, and the countercultures of America. He was a natural for the drug business and knew all the players; the users, the dealers, and, more importantly, the bosses. People trusted him because he wasn't a threat, or at least he didn't seem to be.

"Mr. Santiago, I found him."

"Talked to me, Blackie."

"He's in Mississippi. A city named Biloxi."

"Keep talking."

"You know that Porsche you arranged for Gordon to drive. The one he wasn't paying for and was still registered to the dealer? He traded it in, or rather swapped it out for a new one. Since he didn't have a title it went straight to a chop shop run by the Dixie Mafia. They're teamed up with the Simon City Royals here in Biloxi. Nasty white guys. They reached out to us. A Royal traced it by using the VIN number that I sent out to our contacts. They want the reward. Only had a little body damage, I had it fixed. You know, boss, we send these gangs a lot of coke, and I mean a lot. Had to promise them a couple extra kilos as the reward if that's okay "

" Keep going, Blackie," Santiago demanded.

"I flew out here and found Gordon at the casinos. Gambling's legal and he wasn't hard to spot. Followed him to a place north of town. He's alone, far as I can tell. Mostly staying at the casinos. He does go out to that house for something, though."

"Enough, just kill him."

"Probably not such a good idea, boss. Let's wait. Something is going on. I think he might know how to get your property back. Maybe wait till after the meeting. See what he does. See if he shows. See if he comes through with that widow. I'll keep an eye on him for you." Blackie waited.

"You better be right. I'll sit tight here in Houston. Then we end this one way or another. You keep an eye on that snake and keep me updated to the minute. Anything changes, and I mean anything Blackie, call me immediately. If I don't hear from you, I'll see you at the meeting," Santiago hung up.

Blackie closed his eyes and gathered his composure. He looked out at a petrochemical plant from his hotel window and missed the beauty of his chosen country, Mexico. He wanted more. It was now or never. He turned on his computer and opened Skype.

The picture connected. Three long-stem roses appeared on the screen. They were tied together with a velvet blue ribbon. One yellow, one red, one white. Blackie had talked to this screen many times before. He knew that the man behind the roses saw him, but he also knew that he would never know who this person was. The only face he would ever see was those stupid roses. This man had helped him many times in the past. He had warned him that he walking into a trap, saving his life. He had delayed him at an airport making him late to a meeting that was raided by the Federales, saving him years in jail. Once, money had magically appeared in his account, allowing him the resources to get out of the country. He had also hurt him in the past, leaving him tied up in a building for three days. Blackie knew it was this man, because he always left his calling card, three roses.

A gruff voice came over the computer speakers "Right on time. What ya got?"

Blackie knew to keep it short and sweet. He said, "I found Gordon."

"I already know that. You're in Biloxi. Tell me something I don't know."

"Santiago's in Houston. The meeting is on."

Chapter 23

The Polygon Commission

The Polygon Commission's purpose was simple: To act alone, or in concert with others, to achieve desired objectives and results. Its ultimate goal was to keep their clients at the top of the food chain and among the richest humans on the face of the planet. This was not a hedge fund. To compare the Commission to this relatively new phenomenon would be like comparing brain surgery to a haircut. Their objective was to dominate the world's natural resources, control the value of currency, set monetary policy, and manipulate public opinion. Their purpose wasn't evil. It wasn't complicated. Make money everywhere in the world through the manipulation of governments, money, resources, and power. It was an ongoing effort. The 1% of the 1% of the 1%. A small club.

Four men sat at a table discussing the various solutions and options they would take as they moved through the pre-approved agenda. Another man listened to the plans in the making from across the room, but chose to remain silent, only speaking when a vote was called. These five men were the Polygon Commission, or the Commission for short. Each of the five represent an intricate piece of the whole and has unquestioned authority to bind their group to any course of action agreed-upon.

Mike O'Neal's group represents the financial world. Banks, money, insurance, brokerage firms, and the world of commercial transactions. Nothing more than ink on a piece of paper that can topple governments or control wars. His power, staggering. His payroll, enormous. His intuition of world markets, uncanny. He likes to fix people problems "the old fashion" way. Everyone in the group pretends they don't know what he means by this. He knows they do.

Randy Jones's group is hands on. They represent transportation and communications. This group can cause the shutdown of normal business operations in China, can see to it that a coffee shop goes international, or that satellites go down during your favorite television drama. It's supercomputers grinding data. It's shell corporations owning majority shares of multinational companies. The control of inventory distribution and communications that affect every business, even mom-and-pop shops. A spider's web where only the spider knows where to walk. Wait for the money to stick then devour it. Randy's the captain and always says, "It's a no-brainer and gives me plenty of spare time to fish and hunt anywhere in the world."

Gene Weber's group forges the working man's arrow and the professional man's eyesight. They control jobs and wages, the human factor. His power influences what countries manpower will migrate to, where the jobs will be, how much the people are paid, and to a great extent who is going to be hired. As a direct consequence of his power, this group decides where and who will build the great projects of mankind. Gene maintains in-roads to every labor union, co-op, municipality, assembly line, and production facility on the planet. Within the group, he employs the smallest number of people but requires the largest amount of cash. He spreads it around and it pays back in spades. Gene says it's fun to delegate in small packages filled with large denominations.

John Starke represents the group that controls land; oil, gas, and the management of real property. Land owned and controlled since the days of kings and queens, sheiks and pharaohs, or aquired when New Worlds were settled. Oil and gas revenues are huge but are considered just another tick on the timeline of human existence compared to the raw land. The philosophy is, "They aren't making any more land. Build what is needed today. Then tear it down and build what is needed for the future. Not complicated if you never sell the dirt." Most of the day-to-day management of this group is contracted out to real estate management firms, oil companies, and architectural groups. Overhead is staggering but this group has massive cash flow without much manipulation. The 10% real estate game leaves Uncle John with time to take on special projects that suit his military background.

Alan Calaway is the salt of the earth and the chairman of the commission. His group interacts with the smaller partner groups throughout the world. His secretary speaks twelve languages and maintains offices in every major city in the world. Alan's group also oversees agriculture and mining. Basic human necessities ranging from cattle and fish to water and wheat. Common and rare earth metals, everything from tin and copper to cerium and uranium. His group can change daily eating habits, control manufacturing outputs, or dictate what it costs to make a computer chip. Everyone counts on him for answers and he always has one. He is the driver, whether it be the cart on the golf course, flying jets, racing cars or steering the Commission.

The Polygon Commission started as one member of a three-member group. The group's old world name was Kratos, dating back to before Christ, with a written history going all the way back to ancient Greece. It dates back even further, but there are no written records to prove it. The three groups within Kratos were originally named Bia, Nike, and Zelus. Their founders became the conquerors of the old world.

Kratos evolved through the ages as their tentacles grew. Century after century, they shape-shifted and adapted to the ever-changing world. Their empire continued to grow. In the 19th century, all three groups merged into one: the Polygon Commission. They restructured worldwide and split management into these five cohesive groups.

Smaller groups and individuals help round out the Commission. They are a means to an end and come and go. Used for special projects or for a special purpose, they enjoy what is pitched as a beneficial ride of easy money, or power to feed their ego. The few invited to participate are often ensnared like young virgins on prom night. If severed out for cause, they are often eaten like a male praying mantis after the sex. There are no guarantees, but the lure of business proposals with the Commission can be intoxicating on a grandiose scale.

The five groups work in unison. Bad blood doesn't exist, it's bled out. They funnel money from every business and every basic human necessity in the world into their coffers. It has been long established to take the money up front, before anyone else turns a profit or makes a dime, and to never ever take their eye off the long-term goals. If you drink a cup of coffee in the morning, start a car, place an order on the Internet, fix your house, invest in stocks, pave a road, or even go on vacation, the Commission takes a slice. They don't take much out of every dollar, but pennies on every dollar adds up, and it never stops. Their fingers branched out in every direction where money is made, paid, earned, or invested. Nothing is taboo. They don't play God, they print the bibles. They aren't old money, they are the money. A time-honored business model that controls the majority of the world's wealth and basic resources, with the Commission at the helm. And the agenda continues, uninterrupted. Seemingly impossible, but made simple by control from the beginnings of civilization.

Anonymity is paramount. Only a few people on the face of the planet know, or care, who really controls, makes or manages this wealth. Today the benefactors often live lives that are so opulent they turned to philanthropy, withdraw into seclusion, or burn out in a blaze of glory. Balance sheets are sent out, but the untraceable income streams are distributed at the sole discretion of the Commission.

One such stream is drugs. Throughout history the drug trade has always been easy cash and there's plenty of it. Just another day at the office for the Commission, supply and demand. In today's reality, it is simple competition for their tobacco, booze, and pharmaceutical interests. The feel-good business, as they called it, is not going anywhere, never was and never would. The legislation of morality was always good for the Commission. But the multi-millions in weekly revenue generated from the feel-good business pales in comparison to the groups' true interests and it is only considered a petty cash account. They also know that once it is legalized, the cash profits will dry up and their place in this market will become just another taxable income stream. The big picture dictated when, not if.

The Commission kept their eye on them, but Nate and Sara were not a priority, just another "i" to dot and "t" to cross.

Chapter 24

An Offer You Can't Refuse

" The Beauvoir Estate is a plantation located on the coast of Biloxi, Mississippi. The name Beauvoir means "beautiful to view." It was the post-war home of the President of the Confederate States of America, Jefferson Davis and now serves as the Presidential Library for the former President. In past glories the plantation operated to cultivate cotton. The plantation consists of a Louisiana cotton-style plantation residence, botanical garden, a former Confederate veterans' and widows' home, a Confederate Soldier Museum, the Jefferson Davis Presidential Library and Museum, various outbuildings, and a historic Confederate cemetery which includes the tomb of the Unknown Confederate Soldier. The house is surrounded by cedars, oaks and magnolia trees and at one time had an orange grove behind it. The artesian spring on the grounds feeds the Mississippi Sound that runs across the property behind the main house. The home faces the Gulf of Mexico and Spanish moss hangs from the many large oak trees on the estate.

President Davis died in 1891 and in 1898 his daughter sold the Beauvoir Estate to the Sons of Confederate Veterans. From 1903 to 1957 approximately 2,500 veterans and their families lived at the home, many buried in the historic Confederate cemetery. It was in a cottage near the main house that President Jefferson Davis wrote his memoirs, "The Rise and Fall of the Confederate Government." [1]

The cottage on the Beauvoir Estate is where Sara had agreed to meet Gordon. The voice, however, changed the agreement. Sara was instructed to travel with a stranger to Gordon Manners' safe house, just north of Biloxi. At the same time, Nate was sent to meet with Gordon, taking Sara's place. As always, the instructions given by the electronic voice were unyielding.

Nate sat in this historic cottage gazing at a portrait of the former President Jefferson Davis. He sat with his back to the front door as he had been told. He sadistically looked forward to seeing Gordon's reaction to his resurrection but at the same time, he was worried about Sara's mission. Sara and an escort had gone to Gordon's safe house to search for whatever it was Gordon now possessed and the e-voice (as they now called him) wanted.

Sara's white male escort was a lanky, towering man and he showed up in the hotel lobby dressed in a black suit, black shirt, black shoes, and a black belt. He was clean shaven and had a crew cut, Marine style. When they met in the lobby of the hotel, he did not speak. The man in black approached Nate and Sara and merely pointed to a car parked under the porte-cochere in front of the hotel, gesturing for Sara to walk with him. As Nate watched the two exit the lobby, a numbness crept through his body like he had just been given anesthesia. A surge of lightheadedness and nausea hit him in full force. For the first time since Nate had come back

---

[1] Wikipedia.

from Costa Rica, they were separated. When Sara looked back at Nate before getting in the stranger's black Mercedes, her gaze said it all. Her face spoke of a terror and doubt, yet an understanding that this was the path they had to follow, showing a realization of peril, disbelief, and uncertainty over the situation they were now submerged in. She closed the door to the Mercedes and pressed the palm of her hand against the window as they were separated by a stranger dressed all in black. Nate wanted to run after her and give her one last touch as if it would be his last. The physical pain that followed the numbness was acute. He could feel it without question, but he couldn't pinpoint exactly where it was coming from.

After the Mercedes disappeared into the stormy horizon, Nate turned his attention to the e-voice instructions for himself and drove from the hotel to the Beauvoir Estate to meet Gordon. Now in place at the grand estate, he tried to put Sara out of his mind by convincing himself that she would be alright. He turned his focus to the mission at hand. He couldn't wait to see the shock on Gordon's face as he patiently waited in the cottage, seated with his back to the only door. He watched the entrance by looking at a reflection of the door in the glass portrait of the defeated President of the Confederate Army.

Gordon walked through the door, closing it as he entered the cottage. Nate watched his reflection in the glass. Gordon's demeanor and dress oozed the incorrigible attitude that he had about this meeting; overconfidence. When the door closed, Nate turned to face Gordon. When Gordon saw him, Nate watched as his cocky attitude immediately withered and he turned to run. With one hand on a chair and all his weight on his right foot, Gordon pushed off the chair and bolted for the door. The chair slid out from under Gordon's hand and he fell to the floor, face first. Nate watched Gordon scramble to his knees and try to crawl toward the door. It reminded Nate of a train wheel spinning on a railroad track, steam spewing. Nate ran over and pressed his foot into Gordon's back with all his weight. It slammed him down on the floor as he dug his heal between Gordon's shoulder blades as hard as he could. Nate wanted to kick him in the face but held back, barely. He held him down until he felt Gordon stop and finally surrender. Nate let Gordon roll over. He could interpret the shock in Gordon's eyes. His face said it all. Nate was alive? What was he doing in Biloxi? Was he there to kill him? Disoriented, Gordon's sails lost all wind, his shoulders slumped and he stared at the floor. Nate grabbed him by the hair, turned a chair around with a loud screech made from the tile floor, and threw Gordon into it.

Nate leaned forward and spoke to Gordon.

"Hello, partner. At least I thought we were partners. Maybe even friends?"

There was no response from Gordon. He merely stared at the floor, his face void of purpose. His light khaki suit, pink shirt, and burgundy loafers now void of their purpose to impress Sara.

"I've never known you to be at a loss for words, Gordon. Where is that oratory gift of yours now? Do you remember what you told me when we first partnered up? Do you, Gordon?"

After a moment of hesitation, Gordon shook his head, no.

Nate laughed, "I seem to recall you saying something along the lines of 'partners don't have to be friends, but they always have each other's back.' Isn't that what you told me oh so many years ago? Shit, Gordon, why do all this? The money was flowing. We had a bird's nest on the ground. You didn't do any work. I had the clients paying out like rigged slot machines!"

Nate waited for a response but received none. He kicked the chair. Gordon looked up with glassed eyes. Nate wanted to take a nine iron and tee off in his balls. Work him over with a baseball bat, start at the knees, break a few ribs, and shatter his jaw.

The voice said, "Don't lose it, we need Gordon in one piece."

Nate demanded an explanation. "Why don't you start at the top, Gordon," he growled. "If you leave out one fact, tell one lie, the cops will be here before you can worm your way out. And in the time it takes for them to get here I'll see to it that you need the paramedics."

Gordon remained silent. Nate controlled his rage, remembering the instructions. He changed his tactics and pretended to be vulnerable, saying "We can still be partners in this. Tell me the truth about what's going on and we can get a game plan." It worked.

A twinkle returned to Gordon's eyes as Nate spoke words of compromise. Nate knew Gordon saw his kindness as a weakness, a crack in his armor. He watched Gordon's eyes plot a defense.

Gordon spun his yarn, "I thought the clients were legit. Who knew they were drug dealers. All this talk about bonds, what's that about? I'm worried about Sara. We're all victims here."

Gordon collected himself and looked Nate straight in the eye before saying, "I got a way out."

Nate threw his hands up in surrender and cried out, "Unbelievable! Do you think I am going to believe that bullshit? Even if I didn't know the truth, I still wouldn't believe that half-cocked fairy tale. There's just no end to it with you, is there? I'm the guy they tried to kill! Remember? You're unbelievable!"

Gordon offered Nate a quizzical glance and asked, "What are you talking about, Nate? You can trust me."

Nate's brow drew tight as he ground his teeth. He clenched one fist next to his face and reared back. He stopped short of a blow to Gordon's face and shook his head in dismay. Instead of laying waste to Gordon's face, Nate repeated what the e-voice had instructed him to say to Gordon.

"Listen, Gordon, here's what you are going to do and why."

Nate followed the e-voice instructions. "Get the bonds, get the flash drive, set up a meeting with Santiago Valenzuela in Houston and we give him back his property. All of it."

Gordon stammered, "Sure, Nate, sure. I'm only trying to do the right thing here."

Nate couldn't reconcile with Gordon's complete insincerity, but he stuck with the program regardless. "In return, I have a buyer for your Picasso. My source will give you a perfect forgery and five million, wired in your name to a secure bank account. Plus they'll let you live. Arrange the meeting with Santiago. Afterward, you go back to your wasted life and pond-scum practice with more cash than you would have gotten from your little scheme, plus a fake if you want to try the insurance gambit again. If it were up to me, I'd bleed you out until you told me the truth, but fortunately for you, it's not up to me."

"One problem, Nate. You can't spend money if you're dead. If I meet alone with Santiago, that's what I'll be, dead. If he sees you, you'll meet the same fate," Gordon said.

Nate continued, "Sara will be there to see you hold up your end, not me. My source assures our safety. They have the resources. I know this for a fact, not that I give a damn about what happens to you."

Gordon answered, "So, me and Sara both meet with Santiago, with your source as protection, and we just give him back the property? Doesn't that sound a bit too easy?"

Nate reiterated, "You have something Santiago wants, Santiago has something the source wants. My source swaps a fake Picasso for the real one and gives you money. A lot of it. That sweetens the deal to motivate your greedy heart. You and I, we're just the messengers, the pawns. You know the old saying, don't shoot the messenger? That's us. And Santiago cannot know about our source. If he finds out you are no longer useful to him… well, you get the rest."

Gordon mulled this over for a few seconds before stating, "I'll need the money for the Picasso before we meet with Santiago."

Nate stepped back from Gordon, answering, "They'll be in touch. Call me when the meeting is set up."

Nate had to use all his willpower not to beat Gordon to a pulp. He took a breath and exited the historic Confederate Presidential cottage.

Chapter 25

Man in Black

The weather was taking a turn for the worse. The tropical storm was heading straight for Biloxi with landfall expected by late tomorrow afternoon. Sustained winds were reaching 15 miles an hour with gusts of up to 30, and the rain was falling sideways. Sara sat in the passenger seat watching the sun go down as the wipers slapped the rain from the windshield in rhythmic time. The silent man in black sped down the dark, wet roads, heading north to Gordon's safe house. Sara tried to make conversation, but it was a futile effort. The silent man gave no response and stared forward, looking relaxed as he drove through the downpour. The only response Sara could get out of him was an occasional nod of his head or a quick sideways glance.

Sara became more and more uneasy as the dark scenarios took hold of her subconscious. She tried to get comfortable, she tried to relax, but no such solace would come. She was tormented and started to doubt herself as she sat alone with a stranger, speeding through the night. Sara fidgeted in her seat and checked the time on her watch for the eighth time in the past twenty minutes. She rubbed her palms and pulled her hair back in a ponytail using the hair tie she always kept around her wrist. She straightened her blouse and fidgeted in the seat; nervous habits she resorted to in order to stay in control of her senses, remain calm, and keep her panic in check. Sara sat still for a moment. She embraced her fear and focused her energy, trying to find the strength she needed to keep from jumping out of the speeding car, taking her chances in the woods, and fleeing into the night. She just wanted this endless nightmare to be over.

The car turned off the main blacktop onto a tree-covered side road so thick with oaks that they covered the sky and dropped raindrops onto the car in loud knocks. Sara felt like she was shooting through a tunnel on a roller coaster, headed to a spiritual world in another reality, while the tires made a ghost-like hum from the rain, the windshield wipers keeping beat to a song long forgotten.

"How much longer?"

"We're here," he responded as the car turned into view of a circular driveway.

"Get on the floorboard and don't look up. I will be back in a minute."

The man finally spoke in a full sentence, Sara thought as she unbuckled her seat belt and slid to the floor. She felt the car turn in a half circle around the driveway and slide to a stop. The silent man jetted from the car, leaving it running, and his door wide open. The damp night air washed over Sara as she crouched out of sight, the eerie silence interrupted by the rain pattering on the leather of the driver's seat. Sara softly repeated the Lord's Prayer as she knelt on the floorboard, ignored his orders, and peaked over the dashboard.

The man in black moved up a set of wide red brick stairs that led to a double door framed by two ornate gas lanterns. The steps went up a slight slope, lined with well-trimmed greenery and lit by soothing solar lights. The house was two stories of solid glass, with a matching red-brick front porch running the length of the entire front. A round green copper roof shielded the entrance from the rain. The man moved with speed so smooth and natural that it would appear like a leisure walk in the park to the untrained eye. Most people would have to run to keep up with his comfortable, gazelle-like gait. Moving toward the front door, he slipped on a pair of surgical gloves and then reached into his front pocket, retrieving a key. He inserted it into the solid cypress door and pushed it open.

*   *   *

His eyes never stopped moving as he surveyed his surroundings, digesting every pixel of what he saw as his brain processed them. Every sound, every object, every shadow, and every light were instantly analyzed, mapped, and squared for a reaction by his senses. Precision was forged into his lifeblood through years of training and experience. Stepping across the threshold, he instantly moved in front of an alarm box, opened it with the flip of his finger, and punched in the security code. The light in the box turned green. Success. He then moved deeper into the house, down the foyer, and into the study. It was decorated with mahogany paneling, built-in bookshelves, and a Persian rug lying in front of an antique desk, placed under two overstuffed red leather chairs. He sat down behind the desk, stroked the computer keyboard, and studied the feeds displayed on the monitor by the security cameras. He questioned why people spent such an exorbitant amount of time and money on security systems that were so easily circumvented. A common thief would only need rudimentary knowledge to take everything he wanted.

He pushed a flash drive into the computer that reset the backup time and images on the security system. The backup footage was looped to a time before they arrived and their visit erased. They would be long gone before the images captured by the cameras returned to real-time surveillance. Task completed. The man in black lifted himself out of the black swivel chair and dialed his phone. The other end picked up saying, "How's she doing?"

"Jury's still out," he responded.

"Where are you at?"

"Finishing in the house, going to get her out of the car."

"Has she cracked up yet?"

"No. Doing better than I thought she would."

"Lamb or lion?"

"Too soon to tell, night's still young."

"You think she's got what it takes?"

"We'll see. Let me finish with her and I'll write a full report."

They hung up and he headed to the car to complete Sara's interview.

This man was a soldier on a mission. He didn't need her help, his orders were to evaluate Sara. He was testing her composure, how she handled the unknown, how she reacted under pressure. The man would write a report when the night was over, knowing his employer had other designs for Sara. is report on Sa They had kept an eye on her all her life and tonight was the final exam, pass or fail. The interview proceeded.

*   *   *

As the man opened the car door to retrieve Sara, he spoke."Follow me. Quit worrying. This won't take long and it will all be over before you know it. Just keep up and do what I ask."

As Sara unrolled herself off the floorboard the man opened the rear door, reached in, and grabbed an aluminum case.

What choice do I have at this point? she thought as the rain soaked her clothes.

Sara had to half trot to keep up with the man as she followed him along a flagstone walkway that wound around the side of the house to the rear. He abruptly stopped her with an outstretched arm one step before she would have fallen through an open doorway into a dark hole. Sara looked over at the man in black and followed his eyes to the ground. There, lying at her feet was a flight of stairs descending down into the ground. There was a faint red glow coming from the bottom. It could have been a basement, except it wasn't attached to the house.

Some kind of root cellar? Sara imagined as the man flowed down the stairs, Sara lagging behind. At the bottom, she stood staring at a concrete wall with an oval metal door that had a steel wheel mounted in the middle. It reminded Sara of a submarine hatch. Next to the door was a tiny illuminated pad. She watched as the man pressed what looked like an eraser over the glowing red light. The red light turned green. Next, the man turned the round steel wheel until it made a finishing metallic clank. He pulled the hatch door open and motioned for Sara to go in. She froze.

The man's voice was soft, calm and reassuring when he spoke to Sara. "It's alright. The lights are motion activated. Step inside, they will come on automatically."

"After you," Sara motioned in her best southern Annabelle style, slightly curtsying and sweeping her hand in an arch toward the dark hole.

"I do love a lady with southern charm" and to Sara's astonishment, the man smiled as he stepped through the hatch.

As the lights blinked on, Sara followed the man through the now neon-lit doorway. She squinted and blinked, trying to force her eyes to adjust to the light, but she was, for the moment, blinded. As her eyes adjusted, she looked down a long hallway leading from the entrance. The hall was lined with half-empty shelves and bunk beds that folded up against the walls. She focused and saw a much larger room at the end of the hall. Without mistake, the larger room resembled living quarters and a kitchen.

"A bomb shelter," she whispered.

As Sara's eyes at last fully adjusted, she saw the man kneeling at the far end of the large room. He pulled back the carpet, and she watched in awe as the man in black reached down and pulled open a cabinet door in the floor.

"This way," his voice echoed.

"How did you get there so fast?" Sara called out as she traversed the hallway.

"Keep up, Sara," the man in black replied.

Sara hurried down the hall and kneeled next to the man as he opened the case he had retrieved from the back seat of the car. She looked down and saw an open floor safe, inside of which contained two manila envelopes, a bundle of cash, and a handgun. Sara could no longer stay silent as her motherly instincts took hold.

"What are you? A master thief, a safe cracker, a part-time mime? Tell me that wasn't an infrared fingerprint scanner on the front door of this, what? Bomb shelter? What did you do in the main house? I saw you go in. Why am I even here? Maybe we could start with a short conversation? Start with two sentences that aren't a command and put them together at the same time. It's called a two-way conversation. I need some kind of explanation. Now!"

The man did not respond. He reached down and put the gun from the safe in his jacket, replacing it with another that looked exactly identical. He then removed two envelopes from the aluminum case. He gave more orders.

"Sara, grab the envelopes out of the floor safe."

Sara only glared back at the man in black.

The man repeated himself, "Sara, reach down and get those envelopes. We need to go. Think about Nate and your boys. There, two sentences. Now if you would be so kind."

Sara was still in "mommy" mode, and, in defiance, questioned, "And if I won't, then what?"

The man stopped, not a muscle moving in his entire body. All expression drained from his face and there was a void of emotion behind his eyes.

In a low tone, he answered, "Then Nate's dead."

Sara froze, fighting the urge to cry.

Expressionless, the man continued, his voice coming out of nowhere, "You want a conversation? How about the one where you and Nate are in over your proverbial asses. Your heads are on the chopping block. The less you know for now the better. I'm the solution, not the problem. And that's just the way it is. But, just so you won't go away with nothin', I'll give you some valuable advice. Trust me and do what I ask. The people helping you do not play games and they have very little patience."

Sara felt ice course through her veins and goosebumps ran down her body. She reached down into the safe and pulled the two envelopes out.

The man nodded, "Hold them up and turn them around."

Sara turned them in her hands.

"Now show me what's inside."

Sara complied.

The man gave more orders. Sara did as he asked. She handled the envelopes as the man checked them inside and out, but never touching them. And when he was through, he only said, "Good, now put them in the case."

Sara concentrated now. She turned and placed the envelopes in the precut foam lining of the case. The strange man closed the safe, threw the carpet back on top, and was halfway down the hall before Sara could stand up and follow.

"Wait up, partner," Sara's voice echoed.

The man stopped at the doorway and bowed in his best southern gentile style. He waved his hand in an arch, motioning her through the door, up the stairs, and out into the rain.

"After you," he said in a chivalrous southern accent.

Sara was taken aback but didn't hesitate. She heard the metal door close and lock behind her as the man passed her on the stairs, moving as graceful as ever in his fluid style.

"*Surreal*," Sara reflected, struggling to keep up.

Wiping the rain from her face she ran to their getaway car parked in the driveway. As it came into view she saw it was still running, with three doors wide open.

Chapter 26

Mañana

The Biloxi coastline is inspiring. White sands, gentile mansions, and ancient mossy oaks line a seaside drive. The old southern charm, long stamped out by the sin of a nation, somehow remain on this shoreline, symbolizing a legacy to purity clothed in a past of false innocence. The shadows of this once self-proclaimed great nation are now dominated by neon-lit casinos, souvenir shops, and fast food chains. The approaching tropical storm unleashed the spirits in the form of wind and rain, a reminder of haunting ghosts that can never change the past.

Gordon was still on the fence when it came to who's plan he was going to follow. Nate's, Santiago's or his own. Gordon dialed Santiago Valenzuela from the car on his way to the Hard Rock Casino. After seeing Nate alive he changed his mind about his exit strategy.

"What the hell. I'll make a quick stop for a little gambling, knock back a few drinks, and stay the night. I'll go back to the homestead in the morning to pick up the booty and fly the hell out of here. Good thing I left the Picasso at the beach rental on Boliver Island, not an impossible trip from the airport.

"But first, priorities. Gambling, alcohol, and a roll in the hay. Not necessarily in that order."

Gordon looked down and pushed "send" on his steering wheel. After two European phone rings and several short clicks, Santiago's voice came over the Bluetooth.

"When we meetin', Gordy? I pray it's soon, for your sake."

Gordon came back, "It's all set. Sara's heading back to Houston in the morning. She's agreed to get together and put an end to your dilemma. How do we proceed, jefe?"

Santiago was in no mood to be questioned. "That puta got my property?"

Gordon shot back, "She didn't deny it. Said she needed to get back to resolve this matter. My money says she's got it stashed somewhere in Houston. She was scared after our talk. I made sure to put the fear of God in her. Your plan is working, Santiago. We give her enough rope and hang her with it when we hook up. Heh, no pun intended," Gordon smiled.

Santiago was not amused. "You best be right, mi' amigo. I've come a long way to be disappointed. We'll meet tomorrow at 5. My man here will text you directions."

Gordon, cocky as ever, said, "Looking forward to it."

Santiago finished with, "Bring the woman and my property and I'll let you live, Gordon. Cross me and you will pray for death. Do I need to go into details, my friend?"

"Santiago, come on. We make a hell of a team. Tomorrow at 5 it is. Let's get this behind us and move forward. What do you say?"

All Gordon heard was dead air.

* * *

Santiago took another bite of the fresh quail from the plate in front of him before wiping his mouth with the white cloth napkin. He was dining at Ninfa's Original Restaurant located in the old east end barrio of Houston. It was one of his favorite places in town and he always ate in a private room toward the back. He stood up and kicked the chair he was sitting in across the room. It crashed across the room knocking over tables and chairs with a loud racket. He removed the SIM card from the back of the phone and placed it between his fingers. In a single, practiced motion he snapped the card in two and tossed the pieces on the table. He then picked up the plate and threw it against the nearby wall, shattering it into a dozen pieces.

"Fuck that man!" he yelled.

His guard at the front door quickly moved toward the private room as he reached inside his jacket. Another guard stationed at the backdoor nodded to him, giving him the signal that everything was under control. He confirmed there was no threat and returned to his station. There were two other men seated at the table with Santiago. They never flinched, they were used to Santiago's outbursts. One of them reached into his jacket and handed Santiago another cell phone.

"Gato!" Santiago said in a disquieting voice as he straightened up his shirt. "Tomorrow, this ends."

Santiago motioned for his two men and as he moved toward the front door, they walked in front of him. The man at the rear door covered his flank, while the man watching the front of the restaurant ran to retrieve the Tahoe. Santiago rarely slept two nights in the same bed.

* * *

Gordon wrestled the car out of the weather and into the parking garage at the Hard Rock. This time he dialed Nate's number. Kid Rock's "Cowboy" stopped midway through as the hands-free Bluetooth took over the speakers. Gordon turned down the volume.

"It's on. Houston, tomorrow, 5 p.m. I'll text the location to you when I get it from Santiago. Your source better know what they're doing. We got one pissed off, hot-blooded Latino on our hands. You realize he intends to kill me and your wife, right? Any further instructions from your people?"

Nate answered, "You'll be contacted when you get to Houston."

"Mañana," and Gordon hung up. Kid Rock's "You Never Met A Motherfucker Quite Like Me" came over his car stereo. Gordon turned it up, still uncertain as to whether he was going to make the meeting.

*   *   *

Nate took a deep breath as the phone went silent. He and Sara sat close on the edge of the hotel bed holding hands, each, in turn, telling the detailed story of the other's evening and discussing the latest e-instructions. Nate admitted that he never knew Gordon all that well, and admitted that after tonight he will be taking a whole new look at life in general. As he held Sara's hand, he talked of all his preconceived notions on how he once believed life should be lived. Of how he blindly followed the life models he was taught as a child, his entire life, and how they didn't stack up anymore, and how they melted into false idols of sinful indulgence. Their situation forced him to look at the dark underbelly of living, and priorities were now refocused.

"The one thing I didn't get wrong was you and the boys. That one I got right," he said, slurring his words. "And I'll be damned if I'm going blindly into the night. We need to cover our own ass tomorrow." He let go of Sara's hand and took another long drink of his Wild Turkey and cream soda.

Sara put her hands over her head, closed her eyes and fell back into the soft bed with a calm whooshing sound.

Nate leaned in close and whispered, "I am the master of my fate. I am the captain of my soul. What do you say?"

Sara's eyes shot open, "Oh, get over it! For Christ sake, Nate! Now's not the time to psychoanalyze your babbling bullshit. Your drunk, mister," and she started laughing.

She reached up, grabbed the glass from his hand, and took a heavy drink, continuing, "You've had enough alcohol, fella. Enough already!" She reached over and tickled him. Still laughing she said, "We have a long day tomorrow."

Sara sat up and finished the last sip of Nate's drink saying, "Tomorrow we have to drive to Houston, meet with a cold-blooded killer, avoid death, purchase a Picasso, and piece our lives back together. Quit your wallowing and man the fuck up, Nate." Sara stared at the empty glass and with a slight slur asked "When did we think up this scrumptious drink anyway?"

"Back in the '90s. Remember when all those new drinks were in fashion? We should have bottled it. We would have made a fortune!"

Nate scooted across the bed toward the nightstand where the hotel ice bucket sat next to the cream soda and Wild Turkey. He poured Sara and himself a new drink and raised his glass.

"To buying a Picasso," he said.

They raised the glasses and made a toast to their future, in anticipation of the day yet to come.

Chapter 27

The Crown's Uneasy Mind

A grey-haired man sat across a desk, intently staring at the cards he held in his hand. He was dressed in a hand-tailored suit and a heavily starched white shirt with a red and green paisley tie. His shoes were polished to a black spit shine while his outstretched hand holding the cards flashed his gold nugget cufflinks. His grey hair was trimmed neatly above the ears and shirt collar and his fingernails were recently manicured. He sat back in the desk chair, crossed his right foot over his left knee, and contemplated his next play. His socks, of course, matched his tie.

A second man sat behind the desk and was dressed in similar fashion. His card hand was lying face down in front of him. His once black hair was now solid white, combed back in flowing vogue style. He wore a loud blue and yellow striped tie with a distinct clef in a small knot. The jacket of his blue pinstriped suit hung on the back of his chair. He was kicked back behind the desk in an overstuffed executive swivel chair smoking a cigar. His ostrich-skin cowboy boots were kicked up on the desk and when he reached down for the cards on the desk, his finger sported a titanium ring with a black star sapphire embedded in its center. His cufflinks were one bull and one bear, made of solid silver.

A third man lay stretched out on a white sofa across the spacious office. His grey and white hair thinning, he wore starched khaki pants, a light blue Columbia sport shirt, brown loafers, and white socks. His head was propped up on a pillow with his hands behind his head. He stared at a painting on the wall and spoke

"I don't see what makes that damn painting worth so much money. The value rises faster than insider trading."

He went on in a rhythmic tone, bobbing his head in jest, "I mean, sure, it's rich with color, has great depth, and is from a famous Renaissance artist…" He was actually quoting an art article he had recently read but didn't understand very well. "But come on, it's ridiculous the amount of money someone is willing to pay for that thing."

Neither of the two men sitting at the desk responded. They were all there for a specific purpose, patiently waiting on the call.

When the phone finally did ring, the man behind the desk put his boots on the floor, checked the caller ID, and pushed the speaker button.

"What do you say?"

There were two men on the other end of the phone who spoke at the same time.

The man behind the desk interrupted them, "One at a time, gentle-men. We have three different phones on this conference call. You don't know it, but you're talking over each other and we can't understand a single word comin' outta your mouth. All three of us are present and accounted for on this end."

One voice from the phone returned. "Is this a secure line, Alan?"

Alan, the man behind the desk, came back, "Of course, Mike. Standard protocol, you know this."

The second voice from the phone then spoke to the other unseen caller on the conference call. "You go ahead, Mike. We've already talked, the two of us are in agreement. You can speak for both of us."

The man called Mike was Mike O'Neal, who now had the proxy for the other caller. He came back over the phone.

"Like Gene Weber just said, the two of us are in agreement on this vote, but if the three of you come up with a better plan, we'll gladly consider it. For now, this is our best solution. Move forward. Send Nate and Sara the text we blocked last night that Gordon tried to forward to them from Santiago. Then call our happily married couple and verify they got it. Go ahead and let them know where Santiago wants to meet in Houston. Let's get this ball rollin'."

Gene Weber chimed back in through the speakerphone. "Anyone got a better plan? I'm all ears."

The man lying on the couch stood up, walked across the office, and stood next to the desk so he could be heard when he talked into the phone. "What will this prove? To what end? We have the information back."

Mike O'Neal's voice came back over the phone, "The problem came to our backyard. It's like a UPS delivery to your front door. How many opportunities are we going to get like this? Look, if all goes as planned on your end, no one will be the wiser. Problem solved. Old school is a good school and all that."

The man from the couch, now standing over the phone, looked up and talked directly to the man sitting behind the desk. "You sure about this, Mr. Calaway? We could spin doctor this and still get rid of the problem."

Alan Calaway leaned toward the phone and spoke, "We gotta do this right. We have to be positive about what we do here. It has to go off without a hitch, which means we have to do this ourselves. We agreed years ago that if people might very well die, the decision has to be unanimous. I personally don't see a better alternative. Like I tell my kids, if there is going to be a fight, be the first one there. No harm, no foul."

Alan then spoke to the man sitting across the desk, "What do you say, Randy?"

Randy mumbled something that Alan couldn't hear "Randy Jones, you have to speak up."

Randy Jones grunted. "Mike's a go, but are you sure about this, Gene?"

There was only silence coming from Gene on the other end of the phone.

Alan spoke into the phone again, "Well, Gene Weber, speak your peace."

There was only more silence.

Alan sighed, repeating himself, "You have to personally weigh in on this. Gene, you still there?"

After a moment of hesitation, Gene finally said, "I gotta say, I'm personally tired of that rat bastard. All of you know I voted to kill him years ago and if you'd have listened to me back then, we wouldn't be having this conversation now. I have peaceful dreams of me fragging Santiago in his sleep or tying him naked to my motorcycle and dragging him down some gravel roads. I would find pleasure in it. So my vote is to impale the motherfucker on a stake, up his asshole through his mouth, and watch him shrivel up like a raisin in the sun. It's thoughts like that that help me sleep at night, gentlemen, and if we take out a lawyer or two in the process, I say good riddance."

Alan Calaway interrupted, "I think we can take that as a 'yes' vote, Gene. That's two 'go' votes from Mike and Gene over the phone. What do we three say?"

He looked across the desk again. "Randy, what's your vote?"

Randy nodded his head and spoke into the phone, "I'm with ya'. I say go."

Randy turned his eyes from the phone to the other two men in the office. "What about you two?"

The man standing over the phone in the Columbian shirt spoke first. "I'll vote if Alan votes to continue as planned. I'll go along with everyone if I'm the boots on the ground and I control the op. Which way are we going on this, Alan?"

Alan Calaway put his cigar in the ashtray and straightened up in his chair. He pulled his shirt sleeves down, straightening his cufflinks, and blew the smoke from his lungs across the room.

"You four want to make this into something it's not. Am I the only voice of reason in this group? What's to discuss? We send Nate and Sara to the meeting with Gordon and Carlos, oh, sorry, I mean Mr. Santiago Valenzuela. We made this guy everything he thinks he is today and this is the loyalty we got in return. This guy kills people for fun. He has to be stopped, one way or another. Unintended casualties or not. The stakes are too high and this opportunity is a gift. We will never catch him stateside again."

Alan looked up at the man standing beside the desk in the blue Columbia shirt and said, "If John agrees to run this operation, then it's settled. We're making the right call."

John glanced around the room and finished by saying, "I said I'd vote with Alan. I'm in. I'll run the operation. We move forward." With his vote cast, John headed back across the room to lie down on the couch.

Alan looked around the room, pointing his finger at the phone. "There, we got it. Unanimous. Now that we have our vote, it's showtime. Since all calls that go to Nate and Sara's new phone are routed through us first, we've been able to control their info. We see all their old cell phone and landline calls before they do and we've blocked what we don't want them to get. Gordon sent them a text about the meeting with Santiago, but they haven't seen it yet. We go ahead and let them get that text and send them on their way to Houston. After that, we will call them with detailed instructions. John runs the op. Settled. After the meeting, if Nate and Sara are still on board, we make our proposal, as discussed."

"You mean 'still alive and on board'," one of the men stammered.

Alan sat back in the chair and shouted across the office, "Don't screw this up, John. We could pick a lot worse than Nate and as a matter of fact, we have in the past. Keep them both alive. You've done pretty well so far. As for the rest of you, it is what it is. We all know where this is going. It's a done deal."

Randy Jones responded, "Good talking to me," which was his way of saying *"Goodbye"* and picked his cards back up.

Gene Weber piped in from the phone, "Go fuck yourselves, ladies," and hung up.

Mike O'Neal came on one last time over the speaker, "See you boys in Colorado. Hey, Randy, bring me some Alaskan salmon."

Randy Jones snorted, "Catch your own."

And with that, Mike O'Neal was gone.

The phone disconnected with the sound of a dial tone and Alan Calaway hit the lit speaker button, ending the call. He picked up his cards, put his boots back up on the desk, and with a no-tell stare he searched Randy Jones's face for any sign of what cards he was holding in his hand.

"Your play," Alan said with his best poker face.

Randy Jones glanced down at his cards.

"Got any fours?" he ask with a wily tell.

Alan Calaway glanced at his cards and grinned, "Go fish."

Chapter 28

Houston Or Bust

Nate and Sara loaded the Yukon in the late morning for the six-hour drive back to Houston. There were only the two small suitcases and a small cooler to load up. As Nate closed the rear hatch, he leaned up against the car, rubbing his head. Sara walked over and put her head on his chest, massaging his shoulders.

"Rough night there, cowboy?" she asked, digging deeper into Nate's shoulder blades.

"Great night, cowgirl. Bad morning." Nate put his arms around her and pressed her body up against his.

Sara didn't move and took the moment in with a deep sigh.

"We can do this, Nate. We've come this far and the instructions have been reliable."

Sara backed up and dug through her purse, handing Nate three Advil.

"Here, take these and we'll get some breakfast on our way out of town." She tried assuring Nate he would be fine after he ate something.

Nate gave her a wink as the two turned and walked to the front doors of the SUV. Nate was driving, as always, and Sara took on the role of the reliable co-pilot. They opened their doors and got in the car for what might turn out to be the longest, or last, day of their life.

Sara had to pull herself up to get into Nate's four-wheel drive. It stood further off the ground than a car and she had to hike her leg up and over to get in the door. If she was wearing a skirt she had to pull it up to climb in, oftentimes exposing more than she was willing to share. She was always conscious of perverted onlookers when she climbed into the jacked-up truck. This morning she wore loose slacks for comfortable travel and didn't have to pull her skirt up to get in. She put one foot on the running board, pulling herself up with her hand, and slid her small frame into the passenger's seat. She had done this a thousand times before. When she looked down to straighten up in the seat, she saw the familiar pizza stain on the carpet. She had been meaning to clean it, as it was a new car and all, but she hadn't gotten around to it yet. Remembering how it got there in the first place was a pleasant thought.

One evening, she and Nate had two filet mignons ready to grill. It had been a long day, so they opted for a drink before starting the charcoal grill. One drink led to two, two led to three, and three led to one too many, again. Sara recalled the conversation that ensued.

"Are you still hungry, Nate? If so, you better start the grill," she told him.

Nate responded "Hungry, yes, but I'm too relaxed to prepare a big meal now. Put the steaks back in the fridge. I vote we get pizza."

Sara cared none at this point, so they ordered the usual large supreme with jalapenos and drove the quarter mile to pick it up. On the drive home, Nate reached over for a slice. Sara tried to stop him, resulting in her putting

one large supreme pizza with jalapenos all over the floorboard of the passenger side of the new Yukon. Nate pulled to the side of the road, leaned
across the front seat, and put it all back in the cardboard box.

He then did his best Julia Childs impersonation and said, "You need
to work on your pizza manners."

Sara handed him an already separated slice.

Nate stuffed a big bite in his mouth and muttered, "DWI anyone?"

This morning, as she straightened herself up in the 4X4, Sara realized
the pizza stain hadn't been there on the drive into Mississippi. She remembered dropping her lipstick and thinking Nate had detailed the car. She
looked around the SUV. It was clean, but detailed like she remembered
yesterday, it was not.

"You ready to travel?" Nate asked her as he put the key in the ignition.

"Not yet" as she stared at the Texas registration on the windshield and
exited the car to check the license plates. Nate followed.

"Who are we dealing with?" Sara asked.

Nate followed her eyes blurting out, "They changed the car back to
Texas."

Sara's eyebrows wrinkled. "No. They swapped us back our car."

As they got back in the car, an all-too-familiar ringtone hummed on
the cell phone, a text notification. Nate fumbled with the phone, swiping,
pushing, and punching at it. He squinted and moved the phone in and
out, trying to focus on the display screen. He searched for his reading
glasses. Sara reached over and grabbed the phone.

She breathed deeply. "It's from Gordon."

"What's it say?" Nate asked.

"An address and a time." Sara scrolled further. "The text confirms the
e-voice instructions."

Nate turned the key and started the journey.

"Five o'clock in Houston, Texas, so it is. The instructions yesterday were spot on again. That voice got a crystal ball or something? How does it know what's going to happen before it happens? It's been one step ahead the whole time."

Nate glanced over at the time displayed on the GPS and said, "We can make it in plenty of time."

As the car pulled out of the covered garage he looked around, puzzled, and asked Sara, "Looks like a nice day for a drive, what happened to that storm?"

Sara gazed up at the blue sky, responding, "The morning news said it took a last minute turn east to Tallahassee."

Before Nate's hangover could suffer through any more small talk about the weather, the phone rang again. The Bluetooth was activated and they both listened to the e-voice lay out their daily e-instructions. The e-voice told them their old identities were in the glove-box, along with a pre-stamped envelope to mail their Mississippi aliases. It even told them where the closest mailbox was to get rid of their fake IDs. The voice then verified they got the text from Gordon confirming the time and place of the meet. Its last instruction clarified what to do when (not if) they receive a call from the Houston Police Department.

Chapter 29

If At First You Don't Succeed

G ini sat in the office laboring over the evidence. She was positive she could crack her first murder if she could only find Sara Level or her husband. She was convinced they were on the run together, and once they were found she would connect them to the robbery by tracing their where-abouts and following the money trail. Tie them to the robbery and, hence, the murder. She wanted a conviction and the bad guys behind bars. She had brought a corkboard from home and pinned pictures of the victims, suspects and all the evidence on it. She then connected each picture with yarn she salvaged from her mother's knitting basket. After stepping back to admire her handy work, she was impressed with herself.

O'Hare showed up at the office a little late this afternoon. He pre-ferred the routine 9 to 5, but it was their turn in the rotation for the dinner shift, 1 to 9. It was a random assignment everyone drew from time to time. He usually blamed any tardiness on the morning traffic, but at one o'clock in the afternoon, there was no traffic to be found. No one ever asked or checked on his punctuality, but he was prepared with an excuse nonetheless. Old habits die hard. He was running late today because of an extra long hot steaming shower (and that's not even a good excuse at all). Before coming into work he stood in the shower, letting the hot water run down his body from head to toe. He stood there until all the hot water was gone and his muscles relaxed. He thought about the case as he let the scalding water pour over him, not knowing at the time that it was all now perfectly illustrated on Gini's cork board. The way he saw it, he wasn't late to work at all. He had been working early, one steaming, case-working shower ahead of schedule. Several of his more complex cases had come together when he relaxed in the shower. He knew the department preferred detectives to be thinking about solving cases, rather than wasting time doing busy work at the office. His excuse for the tardiness this day, if only to himself, was he was working out of the office. As he walked to his desk in the station he paused in front of Gini.

"So what's this?" O'Hare asked Gini, pointing at the cork board.

"It's our case board. What do you think?" Gini looked for approval.

O'Hare couldn't criticize. It was a fact that all detectives had their quirks and strange avenues for solving cases. Once he had a lucky hat that he wore to crime scenes for inspiration. He threw it away after his wife told him he just wasn't a hat person, it made his ears look funny. And as far as quirks go, Gini's corkboard was fairly common, with the exception of the different colored yarn.

"Another tenderfoot," he mumbled as he sat down at the desk.

"What's that?" Gini asked.

"The board," O'Hare pointed. "If it helps you organize, I say good work." Gini knew that was not what he said.

O'Hare changed the subject. "You find Nate or his wife?"

Gini concentrated. "Not yet, but it's a new day, or make that afternoon. This afternoon shift kinda throws me off schedule."

"Just be thankful you aren't doing graveyard down in the Third Ward," O'Hare replied. "I can check with my sources and see if there's any word on the street about them, if you think it might help."

Gini felt like she was finally involved in a big decision and turned away from her corkboard.

"Can't hurt," she said, a little too excited to be a part of confidential informant communications.

O'Hare had already checked with his sources and no one had heard of the two Levels. As expected, the street was not part of their scene. He did get an interesting bite from an old CI involved in drug trafficking. The word on the street was there was a major player in town, which equated to a big drug deal. The bigger the player, the bigger the deal, and the word was this guy was top of the heap, A.K.A. a big fish. O'Hare didn't work in narcotics, so he let it lay, but he intended to pass the tip along first chance he got.

O'Hare sat at his desk and worked a few small cases, but he eventually turned his attention to the lawyer condo murder case. As he flipped through the file, something about this case still bothered him. It was too easy, the dead ends too sharp. The case spoke to him, as they all did, and this one said, "Just give me time, I'll solve myself." Unheard of in this line of work, but maybe this was the outlier, the exception. He never heard of any case, much less a murder case, solving itself in all of his years on the force, but there was always a first time for everything.

"No way. What's the catch? Where's the break?" O'Hare mumbled as he flipped through the case file.

Gini raised her eyebrows. "No way, why? What's breaking?" She reminded O'Hare of the introverted smart chick who wore glasses and always sat in the front row of the class.

"You got any new leads on your corkboard case?"

Gini frowned, "No, not yet anyway."

"How about leads on the couple's whereabouts?" O'Hare ran through the routine.

Gini shook her head. "No. There hasn't been any activity at their house and both cell phones still go straight to voicemail. They have to turn up eventually, but I don't think it's a coincidence that they disappeared at the same time as the murder."

Gini had a sudden brainstorm. "What happened with those warrants you were trying to get? Plan on sharing with the rest of the class?"

O'Hare tried not to be impressed but was. He told her the score.

"Couldn't get a warrant to search the Levels' house or his office. To quote Judge Lauren Burkholder, 'It's a law office, for Christ's sake! You got no proof that this Nate lawyer is involved in any murder. You only want to go on a fishing expedition. You got no evidence and no PC. Come back with more than a hunch.' And then the honorable judge ended our meeting with, 'You're not going to cut that fat hog in my courtroom.'"

"That was something my granddad used to say," Gini said with a smile. "I never knew exactly what it meant."

"Obviously you're not a hunter. Judges only go out on a limb so far."

Gini tried to stay on point. "Maybe you want me to dig up something that'll help?"

O'Hare's eyes perked up. "Like what?"

"Well, we got to start somewhere. You want me to take a look at tying the Level's in with some probable cause?"

O'Hare played Gini like a little girl who wanted a new doll. "Maybe this will help you get started," O'Hare reached over and threw two folders on her desk. They were the results of two executed warrants that the Judge did sign off on.

Gini had her new doll to play with after all. O'Hare watched out of the corner of his eye in amusement. Gini eagerly thumbed through the two files thrown on her desk, not knowing that she played right into O'Hare's hand. When she finished, she pushed them aside and looked up.

"Another dead end."

"Why? What are you looking at?" O'Hare was using his teacher voice, which always drove Gini nuts.

She was tired of this class. She became defensive and patronized the seasoned veteran, saying, "Good job on the warrants, O'Hare. You got a warrant for Nate Level's bank accounts, credit cards, and cell phone records. And another one for Sara Level's same info. The results are here, but no leads. Nothing to follow because there is no recent bank activity except automatic withdrawals for monthly utilities, no recent credit card charges, and no recent or even suspicious cell phone calls around the time of the murder. Dead trail. What else ya got?" Gini was clearly frustrated.

O'Hare was patient and explained. "Take another look. There is a lot going on in that information. It's right in front of you. The automatic withdrawals for the utilities were set up after Nate Level faked his death. Like you said, no recent bank account transactions or credit card charges, so they are either dead or in hiding. Living off the land or only spending cash. Maybe on an extended, all-inclusive vacation, but I wouldn't bet the farm on it."

Detective O'Hare picked up the folders and continued, "Let's take this another step. Why be sure the utilities are paid if you're dead? Seems like they have the intention of coming back."

Gini responded with an elongated "Yeeeees. I'm following,"

Then she waited for the rest of the equation. O'Hare was silent, so Gini said, "Sooooo?" and questioned him with her hands and shoulders.

O'Hare went on, "The smoking question here is no cell phone activity. Impossible. If you compare current call activity with past call logs, you see, out of the blue, for no apparent reason, they're not answering anyone's call on the face of the planet. Not just our calls, all calls. And certain people have just quit calling them all together. For instance, their boys. What's up with that?"

Gini's expression soured when she realized what she had missed.

"What's our next move?" she asked.

O'Hare already knew the answer and shared, "Call and triangulate. Find out where the signal is going. Then we can figure out where the Levels are or at least where their phones are. Could be they both ditched them or turned them off. That adds a little suspicion. Or maybe not. But regardless, let's find out."

Gini was all in. "We get another warrant for the cell phone signal?"

O'Hare's patience was that of Methuselah.

"No. We make the call ourselves. We don't need a warrant to track our own call. I've already contacted my man who can track it for us. He's ready when we are."

Gini opened the files back up and studied them with a different frame of mind, thinking to herself, *This sure beats my old days working traffic.*

"I'll call for the trace. You get ready to dial the number. Work for you?"

Gini's face was all business as she said, "I'm good to go."

O'Hare set up the trace and then gave Gini the signal.

Chapter 30

Twist of Faith

Nate and Sara drove the six hours from Biloxi to Houston in what seemed more like one. They stopped only once to fuel up, grab a light snack, and hit the head, as Nate called it. Few words were spoken during the entire trip as they stared at the white stripes painted on the road whizzing by one at a time. Both stayed deep in their own thoughts about the meeting with Santiago, or "the final showdown" as they called it. The possible outcomes were as endless as the sons of Abraham, stars in the night sky, or applications for quantum physics. As they rolled through the armpit of the world (Beaumont, Texas, less than two hours from their destination) they awoke from their five-hour fog and started talking at the same time.

"We have three hours before the meeting…" they said in unison. Usually when they spoke the same thought, at the same time, in the same words, it warranted a smile, a chuckle, or at least the canned response of "Brilliant minds think alike." Today, however, it was just unsettling. It came as a warning of what might appear behind the curtain as it rose for the last act.

Sara broke the anxiety, "Where to now, Saint Peter?"

Nate didn't say a word.

She desperately tried to keep her sense of humor and said, "We could go by the house and clean out the refrigerator."

You could cut the tension with a knife.

Sara trained her worried eyes on Nate. She rambled, "Surely we haven't come this far only to die in an abandoned warehouse at the hands of a Mexican drug dealer, all because of a sociopathic partner while we follow instructions given to us by a mysterious electronic voice from a burner phone."

Sara leaned forward, placed her head on the dashboard, and took a long, loud breath. Her body tensed up and she dug her nails into the seat. The pressure was too much.

"Agggggggggggggggggggggghh!" she screamed.

Nate agreed but kept his focus and said, "What do you say we grab a burger and eat it in Herman Park? Relax a little bit, feed the ducks. It's an easy drive to the warehouse from there."

Herman Park is a 445-acre sanctuary in the middle of Houston, surrounded by the Museum District, the Texas Medical Center and Rice University. Brays Bayou skirts along the edge, adding flowing water and more diversity to the green space. Established in the 1910s, it serves to entertain and relax the population of the nation's fourth-largest city. The park is scattered with tall pine trees, jogging paths, and picnic areas. A zoo, a golf course, and an amphitheater are but a few of the amenities it offers. The reflection pool is home to ducks and is close to the train that toots its high-pitched whistle as it meanders around the park.

Sara wasn't much in the mood for an outing and suggested, "Let's just stop somewhere with air conditioning and wait it out."

Before Nate could concur, Sarah's whole body suddenly twitched in a spasm, a startled reaction from an unfamiliar ring buzzing from a cell phone. Sara reached in her purse and pulled out the phone. The caller I.D. read Houston PD.

"How did they know to program that number in this damn phone?" she asked as she mocked throwing it through the windshield.

They were expecting this call. She answered as instructed and prepared to follow the script.

"Hello, this is Sara," she said pleasantly into the phone.

"Mrs. Sara Level?" the caller lightly questioned.

"The very same."

"Mrs. Level, this is Detective Gini Gibbs, Houston Police Department." Sara heard the shock and surprise in the detective's voice, and also heard a little disappointment.

Sara could have sworn she heard Gini snap her fingers and whisper, "She answered."

Sara waited, giving no response as she followed what the e-voice had told her to say. There were two different sets of instructions given by the voice on how to respond when (not if) the Houston PD contacted them. One was what to say if a Detective O'Hare called; the other was if the call came from a Detective Gibbs. As instructed, Sara waited in silence to let the caller make the next move.

Detective Gibbs finally spoke up. "We've been trying to get in touch with you for some time now. We have left numerous messages at your house and on your cell phone."

Sara gave no response.

"Did you get our messages?"

"We've been out of town. No phone service. Haven't checked our messages since we left. Is everything all right, Detective? What's this about?"

"Sara, where are you? As I said, we've been trying to contact you."

Sara gave Detective Gibbs her rattled, worried voice and answered, "Oh my word, what's wrong? Has something bad happened? Oh my, I knew I should have checked in with someone."

Sara spoke in a high pitch and rushed her words. "Is everything alright at the house? Are the children alright? Please, just say it. Tell me what happened."

Sara played it just as she rehearsed, hoping it was enough to throw Detective Gibbs off her mark.

Sara was told Gini would follow her training and try to calm her. She did just that by saying, "No, no, this is not about your children or the house. Nothing's wrong. We just need to ask you a few questions. Where are you now, Sara?"

Sara eased the tension in her voice. "We took a long overdue vacation. We went hiking the backcountry in Big Bend State Park." She responded, knowing that any lie as to where they had been would be verified. She trusted the voice had covered their tracks and wasn't hanging them out to dry.

"Who is we, Sara?"

Sara came back immediately, "Me and my husband, of course."

"And where is your husband?"

Sara acted put out. She smacked her lips, "Well, he's right here next to me."

Gini was working off a pre-prepared list and went to the next question, "We read that he was dead."

Sara followed the playbook and responded in her panicked voice again, shrilling "Is that what this is about? My husband said it wasn't against the law to have a mock funeral. Was he wrong? I told him it was ludicrous and we shouldn't do it. He said it was to see who was honest, to see if his part-ner would try to take advantage of me. It was all about a new beginning, a new lease on life. A way to sort out his friends from his enemies. That's how he convinced me. Oh my God! What has he done this time?"

"Calm down Sara. I don't know whether it is or isn't against the law to have a funeral for someone who isn't dead. That's not the reason we need to talk to the two of you."

Sara continued with more of her mock confusion. The play-acting was starting to feel comfortable to her as she stuttered, balked, and broke her sentences up. "If your call isn't about the funeral... and everything is... fine... then what is this... about, Detective... Gini is it?"

Sara lifted one eyebrow and squinted up the corner of her mouth, turning her eyes sideways to look at Nate.

Detective Gibbs had tried to be evasive but failed. She glanced up at her corkboard as her planning dissolved like sugar in gasoline. The well-thought-out questions that she had methodically written down were now rendered useless. Sara stayed one step ahead.

"Sara, when can we meet?"

"Why do we need to meet? Please, just tell me what this is all about. You're scaring me," Sara started to cry.

"It's okay, Sara." Gini was flustered now and fell into Sara's hand. "Try and calm down. This is about the murders at Gordon Manner's condo. Routine, but we need to talk as soon as possible."

Sara continued to control the tempo.

"Horrible. We heard. That was horrible. What can we do to help? We're just now getting back into Houston. How about we meet first thing in the morning, say, around nine. Give us a chance to unpack and get a good night's sleep. Does that work? Tell us how you want us to do this."

"Can you come to the station?" Detective Gibbs asked.

Sara jumped on board. "Yes, of course. Anything to help, detective. We'll see you first thing in the morning. Say, nine o'clock sharp?"

"We'll talk then. Looking forward to meeting you two." Detective Gini ended the call.

Sara fell back in the leather passenger seat and looked at Nate. Nothing made sense. How did the voice know all this would happen? Were they getting ready to take a fall for strangers, or would they be led to salvation through acts of blind faith? Did they still have a choice?

"Maybe we can head to the house? Seems safe enough now. HPD isn't looking for us and Santiago has you coming to him. We can wait there until the meeting and any last instructions from the creepy e-voice," Nate said.

Sara covered her face with both hands and all she could say was, "F-I-N-E!" in a loud, long, drawn-out breath.

Before the two could gained their composure, the phone rang again. This time with a familiar ringtone. Sara was positive their calls were monitored. By now she had become so familiar with the ringtone of the e-voice, that she answered it as if talking to someone in the backseat. Sara put it through the Bluetooth as Nate listened with anticipation.

When the e-voice was finished, Sara said, "Got it. It was expected."

Nate followed, "We'll be there and, yes, we will be exactly on time."

Nate turned the car toward their house, actually looking forward to getting this over with and their life back. If they lived.

Chapter 31

The Showdown

Three men entered an abandoned rundown warehouse on the outskirts of Houston through the small steel backdoor. Two of the men were dressed completely in black, SWAT style, with one of them carrying a long Kevlar bag. They were followed by a third man with hearing aids, wearing a blue and yellow Hawaiian print shirt, pleated khakis, and brown tassel loafers. He walked with a cane, carrying a brown leather briefcase and a black easel bag strapped over his shoulder.

The four-story open warehouse was the size of a football field with a large overhead crane in the middle, mounted on an I-beam. The corrosion and decay all around dictated that the crane was no longer in operation, and it probably wouldn't ever be again. Rusted metal grate stairs and catwalks encircled the four stories around the outer perimeter and crisscrossed the ceiling above the crane. Massive concrete columns rose from the floor to the ceiling, lined up like soldiers guarding and surrounding whatever was once in the vast open center of the old warehouse. Eight feet of single-paned windows, once giving light, rolled around the top of the four outside walls, now dirty, broken, and yellowed. The entire end of the warehouse stood open to the weather, the massive doors missing, leaving the concrete floor standing in pools of water, with everything steel now rusting, everything concrete now stained, and everything painted now peeling.

The man with the Kevlar bag set it on the floor and put on a headset, speaking, "How long has this site been under surveillance?"

The second man, already wearing a headset, responded, "Three days now, round the clock. We saw one scout here yesterday, around zero five hundred. Came and went in less than thirty minutes. They weren't professionals. Sloppy tradecraft."

"Where would you set up?" the first man asked, picking up the Kevlar bag.

"It's all an open shot. I'd set up on the catwalk behind the crane, north end. That's the fastest way out of here."

The man carrying the Kevlar bag then turned and spoke to the man in the Hawaiian shirt, "What do you say, John?"

"Be sure of your exit. You need to be out of here, unseen, in less than thirty seconds. You've read the mission statement. Protect the packages, take out the targets if all else fails, but only on my signal. When it's over, right or wrong, good or bad, the lookout will pass by the rear exit. Do a roll into the bed of the pickup. You will be extracted from this area through the abandoned paper mill to the east. It's secure, we have the gate keys," John explained.

The man nodded his head, responding, "Yes sir, that was the briefing. I know my marching orders." He then turned and headed up the grate stairs, Kevlar bag at his side.

John leaned on his cane, straightened his Hawaiian shirt, and turned to the other man.

"We have an active lookout already in place. He's giving us a for-ty-five-second warning. Set us up a second lookout at the Stop and Rob by the freeway. You should be able to give us a little under two minutes' warning of any arrivals from that position. Sound about right?"

The second man agreed, "Affirmative."

John looked around the abandoned warehouse, then back at the man.

"Give us a mike check."

The man spoke into his headset, "This is Leader One. We are less than an hour from party time, gentlemen. Confirm positions. Skyview, you read? Over."

The sharpshooter taking position overhead, behind the crane, re-sponded, "Roger, Leader One, loud and clear. I'm a go. Skyview over."

Leader One spoke again, "Lookout, confirm, over."

The man stationed forty-five seconds from the warehouse lowered his binoculars and spoke through the headset.

"Lookout confirmed. In position. Over."

Leader One spoke once more through the headset. "How about it, Elvis? You in the building? Confirm. Over."

John reached up and messed with his hearing aid, "Roger, Leader One, loud and clear. Confirm reception, over."

Leader One gave John a thumbs up and spoke one last time into his headset.

"We are a go, school girls. Everyone stay on plan, eyes on the ball, over and out."

With those last words, Leader One exited the warehouse and drove away to take up position for a two-minute warning. John waited in the empty warehouse. He found a broken lawn chair and sat out of view behind the stairs. He wanted a smoke, but quickly remembered he had quit years ago. As he waited for the games to begin, he looked across the vast empty warehouse and wondered what kind of fool put innocent lives in harm's way with a vote. Cannon fodder sacrificed for the greater good, according to opinions of people the condemned would never meet. He thought about Nate and Sara being played like chess pieces in a game of life and death, money and power. If they approached Santiago it could go either way. As in life, there are no assurances of success. John went along with this plan, but was now was having doubts. The only other alternative was to do this thing himself, take Nate and Sara out of the equation and go to the meeting alone. He wasn't sure which way he would play it. He would make that call when it needed to be made, on the fly, at the last minute when there was no turning back. To hell with the Commission and the unanimous vote. He would make the call on this one, all on his own.

Time passed at a tectonic pace as John relaxed and anticipated the fireworks. With his eyes closed, he slowed his heart rate as he sat hidden in the broken lawn chair. Right on schedule, his headset sounded.

"This is Leader One. We have a Hertz Rent-A-Car headed your way. Maroon 2017 Mazda. Gordon Manners, sir. Seems to be alone. Over."

A little over a minute later, the man code-named Lookout came over the headset.

"Confirmed. It's Gordon Manners. Forty-five seconds. He's on his way, over."

John took his time standing up while he adjusted the Colt .45 holstered on the side of his pants under the un-tucked Hawaiian shirt. He then reached in the back of his khakis and straightened the 9mm stuck in the crack of his ass.

John moved from under the stairs as he watched Gordon Manners drive his car into the middle of the open warehouse. Gordon stopped and stepped out of the car and into the vast empty space. John walked out into the open. When Gordon saw John he held up a towel draped picture frame and an aluminum hard-sided case. John walked across the warehouse and stood, face to face, with Gordon.

"Is that the Picasso?" John asked.

Gordon barked, "You got my money?"

John stepped forward and snatched the painting out of Gordon's hand. Without stepping back he threw the towel aside, checked what was underneath, and when he was satisfied, leaned it against the car. John was no expert, but what he did know was that Gordon did not have the time to paint a fake. Gordon opened the aluminum case and showed John the bonds, then reached in his pocket and showed him the flash drive. John had him hold them up and before Gordon knew what happened, John sprayed the envelopes and case with a small aerosol spray can. John was satisfied and reached into his shirt pocket without taking his eyes off Gordon. Gordon flinched and tried to take a step back in retreat.

Before Gordon could back up, John grabbed him by the shirt collar, looked him straight in the eyes, and stuffed a piece of paper in his front shirt pocket, saying, "The bank account number and password holding your money are written backward on that paper, every two numbers are transposed, just to be on the safe side . CIBC bank in the Cayman Islands."

"When Santiago gets here, you make the exchange and give him the case. Beg for your life. If anything goes wrong, you're on your own. Screw this up and I'll kill you myself. Questions?"

John let go.

Gordon realized he had no out. "I can do this. You know Santiago wants revenge. If he sees Nate, he'll kill him on the spot. He'll kill Sara, too.

Either right here or he'll kidnap her and kill her slowly somewhere else. It's a Latino thing. He needs to make an example out of her."

John took out a matching Picasso from the easel case he was carrying and swapped it with the Picasso leaning up against the car.

He put his hand on the side of Gordon's face and slapped him before speaking.

"That password to the bank account won't be any good until you've done exactly what you've been told. Exactly. You do understand that, right, Gordon?" John said.

Gordon nodded.

"When the cops want to know what happened, stick to the story the call told you to use. Weave the facts of what really happens into your tale. Leave me, Nate, and Sara, out of it. Do I need to explain why? Or what will happen to you if you don't?"

Gordon's eyes went blank. John patted him on the cheek again.

"Tell me what your instructions are, Gordon."

Gordon repeated what the strange phone voice told him to say. "I was meeting a client. They sold this warehouse and hired me to do the paperwork. He introduced himself as Juan Batista, President of M&M Traders, a South American company. He said he would send a representative to close the sale. The buyer wanted to take one last look at the property and I was meeting both parties here. After this, we were going out for dinner to sign the documents. I never met any of them and don't know who was who. If you don't believe me, I have the paperwork in my briefcase, in the back seat of the car. The buyer and seller were all talking. The buyer opened up a case and the next thing I knew there was gunfire." Gordon took a breath, hesitating.

John gave him a demanding glare. "Finish the story, Gordon."

"I got a good look at them. The men who got away were all about five foot eight, dark hair, Hispanic."

"What else?" John asked.

"Juan Batista said they were interested in buying my Picasso. Thank God they didn't know I brought it. It's in the car."

John then threw the forgery and the small leather briefcase into the backseat of Gordon's car. He turned toward Gordon and said, "Get back in this car and don't get out until you see me walking toward Santiago. You got that?"

Gordon nodded.

When John turned to walk back into the shadows, the easel case tucked under his arm, a voice came through his earpiece.

"This is Leader One. We have Nate and Sara less than two minutes out. Over."

As he moved toward the back door his hearing aid fired off again.

"This is Lookout. Nate and Sara confirmed, forty-five seconds to arrival. Over."

John walked outside the warehouse to wait for Nate and Sara. As they drove up he could see the shock on Sara's face and the puzzled look on Nate's. The car stopped and Sara jumped out. She ran up to him shaking her head back and forth and mouthing words, but there was no sound. John Starke was Sara's Uncle, on her mother's side. He reached out and gave Sara a big hug as she ran into his arms. Nate stepped out of the car at a more measured pace. He walked up behind Sara and stood there with his arms crossed, waiting for the family reunion to get started.

Sara's words found her voice.

"Uncle John, what are you doing here? How is this possible? What's going on?"

Uncle John didn't answer. He looked up at Nate, shook his hand, and said, "You old rascal. I thought you were dead. I went to your funeral and everything. Nice service. I saw you watching from the hill, Nate. Now you know how that phone ended up in your living room."

Without another word, John held Sara's hand, slapped Nate on the back, and led them inside the warehouse. In this moment John made his last minute decision. He was going to the meeting alone.

"There has been a change of plans," he started.

"You two get back in the car. Be patient. Whatever happens, whatever you hear, don't come back in. Just wait. A man will show up and get you the hell out of here. Got it?"

Nate was all business when he replied, "No. I don't got anything. How are you mixed up in all of this?"

John smiled. "You do this one last thing and I will explain later. We don't have the time right now. It will all make sense soon, I promise."

John put his hand up to the hearing aid, listening. Nate thought he was adjusting the volume.

"This is Leader One. We have a Porsche and a Tahoe headed your way. Over."

After listening, John said, "Santiago is almost here. It's showtime," and in his best-imitated e-voice said, "*Do you understand your instructions?*"

Sara's jaw dropped, "You're the creepy e-voice?"

Nate said "We're not going anywhere. We're here to settle this."

As her Uncle, John pleaded, "It's worked out so far. It's not worth the risk. This'll all be over soon. Back to normal, if that's possible. Follow my instructions this one last time."

"Not a chance," Nate said. "We have a different plan. It doesn't change because it's you. It only makes it easier. We do it our way this time."

Sara reached in her purse and handed Nate a .357 pistol he had gotten out of the gun safe back at the house. She then reached back in her purse and pulled out a Browning .380 automatic, jacked a round in the chamber, and put it back in her purse.

"Can those be traced?" John asked.

Nate answered, "No. We bought them at the Pasadena gun show. You know how it works, no paper trail."

"Can I talk you out of this?"

"No." Sara and Nate both spoke at the same time.

"This is Lookout. The Tahoe pulled off to the side of the road. Probably waiting on the all clear. The Porsche is 45 seconds out. Over."

Nate realized the hearing aid was a two-way radio and asked, "How many people do you have watching this meeting?"

"Not enough," John responded and laid out the new plan. "Sara, you walk behind me. I'm your cover. Nate, you back us up from here."

"Nope," Nate interrupted with that word again. "I'm with you. Sara stays here and watches our back."

"It's going to happen fast," John said.

"We're ready," Nate responded.

There was no time to reason with them. John realized they had talked this over and their minds were made up. He watched chills run down Sara's spine as Nate put the gun in his back pocket. He held up one finger signaling them to stay back and moved where he could see into the open warehouse.

The Porsche entered through the missing doors, rolling to a stop behind Gordon's rental car. It just sat there. Three minutes later, John got the broadcast.

"This is Lookout. That Tahoe is startin' to roll. Guess he got the all clear. Over."

Forty-five seconds later, the black Tahoe came through the massive opening and swung around in front of Gordon. Two men stepped out of the back and inched to the front. The driver rolled down his window and adjusted the rearview mirror, to get a clear view of anyone sneaking up from behind. Next, the door of the Porsche swung open and a small, South American man stepped out. It was the Incan, Blackie. He walked over and stood behind the other two.

The air was thick with anticipation as Santiago finally stepped out. He walked around in front of the three men and motioned for Gordon to approach. Gordon stepped away from his car, holding up the metal case. The fear showed in his face, but he obeyed and walked toward Santiago.

Cold as ice, Santiago spoke, "Where's the bitch, Gordy? Promises broken are paid in blood. You know I don't like surprises."

Gordon held out the case as one of the henchmen jerked it out of his hand and gave it to Santiago. He threw it on the hood of the SUV, clicked opened the hasps, and rifled through the contents.

Santiago looked at Gordon with eyes black as coal.

"You got an answer for me, abogito?"

Gordon started to shake. All he could come up with was "Mr. Valenzuela, it's all there, everything she took."

Gordon stuttered "It . . . it wasn't me, she gave me the case and said she would be here... but..." He stopped in mid-sentence, turning around to the sound of footsteps echoing toward him.

Uncle John Starke gave the appearance of a deaf, white-haired old man, on vacation somewhere in the tropics. He had a slight limp as he walked using his cane, hunched over, holding his lower back. Directly behind him was Nate. He walked across the warehouse and stood next to Gordon.

Santiago let out an evil chuckle and reached for his gun.

Chapter 32

The Making of a Hero

The call came in at 4:24 p.m.

Detective O'Hare was working inside the evidence room, refreshing his memory for a trial he had to testify in later that week. The case he was preparing for was over three years old, but he remembered it like it was yesterday. A lovers' spat resulting in the murder of a young woman by her white supremacist boyfriend. As O'Hare held the murder weapon in his hand, the facts came flooding back.

The tattooed supremacist had beaten his girlfriend of eight months to death with a lava lamp. The pictures spread out on the table before him showed the dead woman and the blood spatter patterns from the beating. These patterns displayed textbook savage rage, evidenced by the spatter running eight feet up the two walls behind and beside the bed the victim had been lying on, with some on the ceiling. After beating her to death, the perp placed her lifeless body up in a sitting position on the bed, with her back against the headboard, and then pumped two rounds from a .38 Special into her head. O'Hare was forced to let his tenderfoot in training,

Detective Gibbs, come along and when he showed her the pictures, her enthusiastic excitement escaped her face and she almost threw up all over her brand new, highly fashionable shoes. The pictures said it all and O'Hare figured his testimony wouldn't take thirty minutes. What intelligent, self-respecting defense attorney would keep him too long on the witness stand or ask too many questions on cross-examination, after all. But, on the other hand, the defense attorney was court-appointed and got paid by the day, not by his amount of self-respect or brains.

Gini turned away from the pictures and answered the phone hanging on her belt.

"This is Detective Gibbs," she choked.

"You're with O'Hare," a voice stated. Gini noticed right away this was not phrased as a question. "Put it on speaker." Gini pushed the speaker button on the phone.

"Who's calling?" she asked as O'Hare looked up attentively.

"If you come now, you two can find the person responsible for the murders in the Manners' case. They're meeting at an abandoned warehouse located at 6666 Hargrove Ave. The old warehouse district, Pasadena. It's going down now. More people are going to die, you should hurry," the caller stopped.

"Who is this?" Gini repeated, her eyes squinting into the phone.

"They will be gone in thirty minutes. Consider this a gift from an anonymous party seeking justice. Tell O'Hare that Raymond Hunter says we're even." The line went dead. Detective Gibbs stood stiff and waited for O'Hare to lead.

Detective O'Hare's eyes turned distant, if only for a second, as his mind flashed back to a time and place long before the term "post-traumatic stress disorder" was the politically correct catchphrase for the human price paid for war. O'Hare had stopped Raymond Hunter from killing a man outside a bar shortly after Hunter's return from Vietnam. O'Hare was just a rookie on patrol at the time when he witnessed Hunter raring back with a baseball bat in his hand, ready to release a lethal blow onto the head of another man. O'Hare had recognized the tattoo on Hunter's massive bicep. He was Special Forces, Green Beret.

O'Hare grabbed the bat at the business end and said, "You'll kill him. You're home. It's over."

Being a veteran himself, O'Hare didn't arrest him and saw to it that Hunter got help. The VA didn't publicly recognize PTSD as a type of injury back then, but after support groups, counseling, and the love of a good woman, Hunter finally came home. The two managed to keep in touch for several years after the incident. Hunter always told O'Hare that he had saved his life that night and he would repay O'Hare before he died. Detective O'Hare took this call very seriously. A statement of fact, pure and simple.

O'Hare looked at his watch and bolted from the evidence room to the unmarked squad car. Gini had never seen him move that quick and didn't know he could run that fast. She struggled to keep up.

As O'Hare started the car, he screamed at Gini, "Okay Google that damned smartphone you carry around so much and get me the exact directions to that address."

Gini thumbed the phone, waiting for a response as the fuel injectors in the engine of the car sucked all the fuel they could consume while the windshield lights flashed red, white, and blue. O'Hare pushed the car to the limits. He only slowed down when the car slid sideways around corners or braked for clearance as they blew through every red light. Gini was impressed and saw a new determination in O'Hare that she didn't know existed. She held onto the door and the dashboard, impressed by O'Hare's true skill set hidden beneath all of his daily camouflage.

Google Maps came on the screen and Gini shouted over the roar of the V8. "The address is located off Highway 225 South, left on Richey, right on Hargrove, all the way to the end!"

"I know a shortcut," O'Hare gritted as he turned onto the freeway and pressed the pedal to the metal.

Gini grabbed the handle over the door and watched in motion picture vision, frame by frame, the engine scream and the car gained more and more speed. O'Hare's knuckles turned white as he exited the freeway, jumped the curb and sped bouncing across a field. Gini saw the only mountain in Houston, an eighty-foot spoil bank. The car fishtailed as they climbed and almost flipped as they slid down the steep incline on the other side.

Gini felt the adrenaline rush through her veins. It gave her the high of a junkie getting a fix. She breathed in deep, savoring the intensity for a brief moment, before she radioed the station for backup.

Chapter 33

The Final Draw

Santiago Valenzuela's hand was on the gun, but it never broke leather. The guard's hands were on their weapons as well, waiting on a queue to draw and kill. A wrong move, a hand out of sight, or a verbal threat would justify raining lead. No one moved, everyone stood stone still. One of the guards pulled his jacket back and revealed a .225 automatic assault rifle. He flipped it up on his shoulder as he picked his teeth with a toothpick.

"Target acquired," Skyview spoke into his headset. John waited.

"You bring this as backup, Gordon? The Ghost of Christmas Past and grandpa? Where's your wife, lawyer man?" Santiago asked Nate.

Nate didn't respond.

"She caused me a great deal of trouble." Santiago continued, "She was going to be my hostage, at least until I got all my property back. Then maybe not so much a hostage, more of a guest. I was looking forward to her company. Oh yeah, and since we're on the subject, where's the flash drive, Gordon?" Santiago unholstered his gun with lightning speed and pointed it straight in Gordon's face.

Gordon's voice cracked, "In my pocket, Santiago."

A voice came through John's earpiece, "This is Lookout. That cop found a way around us. He's less than fifteen seconds out."

"Hand it over, Gordon. Slowly," Santiago ordered, still holding his gun to Gordon's face.

Gordon's hand shook as he reached in his pocket and handed Santiago the drive, saying, "I told you everything was under control. We're on the same side here."

Santiago took a step back and put the flash drive in the open case lying on the hood of the car. He started pointing his gun at each person in succession.

"Eenie, meenmi, miney, mo. Who's to die and do I let anyone go?" he hummed, bobbing his head back and forth and moving the gun from one person to the next. He liked playing this game. One of the guards laughed.

"Now would be a good time, John," Skyview sounded into the head-set, but John remained silent.

Then they all heard it. The sound that came out of nowhere. It cracked like thunder, became louder, more abrasive, and was getting closer fast. It was the sound of an engine on the verge of exploding. Blown rings in a racing engine, mixed with the sound of loose metal parts slapping against each other and being dragged on the ground. The acoustics of the ware-house blocked out the sound until it was right on top of them. Santiago's men turned and drew their weapons. Then they all saw it.

*   *   *

O'Hare's cruiser blew into the warehouse like hell on wheels. He locked up all four tires, as the car slid sideways and screeched to a stop twenty feet behind the Tahoe. O'Hare couldn't make out their faces, but he saw at least four or five men pointing guns at them.

"Shit!" he yelled.

As the car rocked to a stop, Gini went for her gun and started to open the door. O'Hare grabbed her and threw her to the floorboard. He jumped on top of her as automatic gunfire riddled the windows and the front of the car. The noise was deafening. Automatic and small arms fire, with glass, metal, and steam going every which way. O'Hare drew his gun and rolled over on his back, staying behind the firewall and on top of Gini. He shielded his eyes from falling debris and positioned himself so he could shoot anyone who appeared in the windows.

*   *   *

The instant Santiago and his men opened fire on the cop car, John reached for the gun stuck down the crack of his ass. Santiago saw him out of the corner of his eye and swung his gun around. He beat John to the draw and squeezed off a round, hitting John in the chest. John crashed backward into Nate and they both fell to the floor. Santiago's gun breached open, he was out of ammo. He popped his spent magazine and slammed another into the gun. Nate saw the 9mm laying next to John and grabbed it. He raised it up and emptied it at Santiago.

Nate hit his target. Hollowpoint lead entered the side of Santiago's head, blowing his forehead, left eye, and ear from his face and shattering his jaw. The brains and flesh splashed onto the side of the Tahoe like a plate of spaghetti thrown against a kitchen wall. His faceless body took one step forward and stood up straight before folding like a Chinese fan onto the concrete. Blackie was the only bodyguard who saw Santiago fall. He quickly ran to the driver's door of the Tahoe and opened it. He pumped two shots in the driver and threw him out of the car. He hopped behind the wheel and floored the Tahoe between Nate, John, and the firefight, shielding the two from the gunfire. The metal case full of bearer bonds flying off the hood and scattering like confetti in a ticker tape parade.

Gordon saw an opening. He grabbed his Picasso out of the rental and charged toward the Porsche. He threw the painting in the back and jumped into the driver's seat. He reached for the ignition but froze at the sound of a click. There was a gun to his chest. He looked up to see Sara staring down at him. She was grinning as she leaned in the car. Keeping her gun pressed against his chest, she calmly removed the keys from the ignition. She leaned back out of the car and, without hesitation, pulled the trigger, pumping a single round into Gordon.

Blackie pushed the button rolling down the electric window as he shouted at Nate, "Grab that old fart and get in! Hurry!"

Nate didn't argue. He knew a gift when he saw one. He glanced around the warehouse to be sure Sara was gone. He then quickly wiped his finger-prints off the pistol and slid it underneath the car toward Santiago's body. He grabbed Uncle John and dragged him into the backseat. The guards continued to fire as they walked backward to get in the Tahoe. Before they could reach it, John and Nate were in the back and Blackie hit the gas and flew out of the warehouse. Nate checked for a pulse.

*   *   *

Sara ran out the back door, heading for her car, but once it came into view she stopped on a dime. There was already a man sitting behind the wheel. With outstretched hands she leveled the gun on the man, keeping her sights trained on him as she moved closer.

The man lifted one finger off the steering wheel and gave her the Texas howdy, then said, "Quit messing around, Sara, I'm with your Uncle John. Time to get the hell out of here." He looked familiar. It was the man in Black.

Sara jumped into the car, out of breath, ordering "They've got Nate and John. We have to go in and get them. We need to rescue them. Now!"

The man in black was cool as ever and responded, "Not to worry. It's all covered, Nate's alright.,"

* * *

"This is Skyview. Requesting evac. Over," was what came over the comms.

* * *

Inside the warehouse the gun battle ensued, but the odds had shifted. O'Hare heard a car speed away and the raining bullets slowed down.

"Stay down, Gini!" he commanded.

O'Hare unfurled off the floor and pushed the door open with his foot. As the door swung open he snuck a quick look over the dashboard through the shattered windshield. He saw two men ready to unload on the opening door. O'Hare didn't flinch. He drew his gun, steadied it on the dashboard and pulled the trigger. One man went down and the other grabbed his leg as he hobbled for cover.

With his gun squared on the target, he exited the vehicle and shouted, "Stop! Houston Police Department! Get on the ground!"

The wounded man lifted the assault rifle as he turned toward the detective. O'Hare nailed him with the first shot. The man went down and never came back up.

*   *   *

Gordon had not moved a muscle. He sat in the Porsche bleeding. The whole incident had taken, in Gordon's mind, less than a minute. He heard faint sirens and pressed his hand over the bullet hole to slow the bleeding. *That bitch!* was his last thought before he passed out.

Chapter 34

Another Dead File

Detective O'Hare lowered his gun and surveyed the scene. Four dead, blood everywhere, paper scattered all around, and Gordon Manners sitting in the front seat of his Porsche with what looked like a bullet wound. Detective Gibbs, on the other hand, struggled to get off the floorboard as she kicked the door open and sprang from the car. She drew her service revolver and used the open car door as cover, shouting,

"Don't move!"

Detective O'Hare gave her a sympathetic glance and in a calm voice told her, "Gini, stand down. It's over. We just have a crime scene now."

It wasn't long before the scene was taped off, bullet casings were marked, and hundreds of pictures were taken. As the bodies were being removed Detective O'Hare worked to piece together what had happened. He took Gordon's statement before he was transported to the Memorial Hermann Hospital in the Medical Center. His statement actually fit the facts apparent at the scene. Detective O'Hare knew there was more to the story, but he also knew he would never get it out of Gordon.

As the last body was hauled away by the coroner, Gini felt successful relief and turned her attention to O'Hare, asking "What do you think, fearless leader?" She placed her hands on her hip and waited for an answer.

"Looks like we get the publicity for one of the most sought-after fugitives in the country. FBI's most wanted, Santiago Valenzuela, dead. Shot during a gun battle in the side of the head. Millions of dollars' worth of blood-soaked bearer bonds littering his grave. This will be one for the papers, no doubt."

Gini piped in, "Don't forget the flash drive. Might lead to more answers in this case."

O'Hare felt like he was wasting his breath.

"Don't bet on it. If you want to place a bet, put it on the 9 mil we found near Santiago matching ballistics with the one that killed the security guard at Gordon's condo. That case, open and shut, or so it appears. Drug-related. This one too."

Gini tried to wind it down by saying, "Must have been a hell of a drug deal. My estimate is right around twenty million in bonds. At least the guys that got away didn't get the booty. We own that one."

O'Hare wasn't amused and all he could think of to say was "Looks like it."

The next morning, O'Hare entered the office to a standing ovation. Everyone was cheering and clapping and a few held up the morning edition of the Houston Chronicle. The headline read: "FBI Most Wanted Apprehended By Houston Detectives." O'Hare found it ironic that the definition of "apprehended" included hiding behind a firewall while a drug lord was shot in a gunfight. He played along anyway, holding both hands in the air for victory as he headed to his desk. He sat down and looked at Gini. She was brooding.

He knew better, but in the spirit of the moment he asked, "What's wrong, detective?"

Gini pointed at the newspaper lying open on the desk in front of her.

"They spelled my name wrong. It's Virginia Gibbs, not Ginny Giggs. No one will know it was me unless I tell them. It's not fair."

"Fair is where you take a pig to win a blue ribbon," O'Hare responded. He figured he'd give her an out and change the subject.

"You ready for Sara and Nate Level?"

Gini came back with a grin. "Yesterday's news. I don't care if the guy buried himself. You said so yourself, they're not killers. To be exact, you said, 'Not their M.O.' I verified their vacation in Big Bend through credit card transactions that just showed up from the warrant. Can't put them at the murder scene. Facts dictate that they didn't have anything to do with it. I'll ask routine questions, but unless something incriminating pops up, I'll have to let them go. Sound like a good exit strategy?"

"How is Manners?" O'Hare asked.

"He's fine. Hard to feel sorry for a lawyer. The bullet went through the shoulder, in and out. Small caliber, clean wound. He's already out of the hospital. The papers for the sale of the warehouse were in his briefcase. He gave another statement at the hospital. It checks out," Gini responded.

O'Hare knew better and said, "We'll catch this guy doing something. It's just a matter of time. Karma's a bitch."

Gini folded up the newspaper, still pouting.

Chapter 35

Small Potatoes

Uncle John Starke lounged in a green leather wing-back chair with buttons holding down the tufted stuffing on the back and seat. The chair was a matched set of two, placed in front of a burl coffee table, centered on top of a hand-woven silk rug. It was a majestic setting, placed in front of a massive river stone fireplace. He took a sip from a cut crystal highball glass filled with three fingers of thirty-year-old scotch. Across the room from this seating area, four men sat at a ball-and-claw black walnut conference table that was inlaid with mahogany and cherry wood. The chairs matched, with the seat cushions made of fine camel hair, red and green striped. They were working from an agenda displayed on a sixty-inch flat screen.

Alan Calaway moved his finger across the tablet in front of him and the big screen TV went blank. He poured himself a drink and leaned back in his chair, savoring the generous sip of his bourbon.

"And that concludes our weekly meeting. What do you say we move on to discuss Nate and Sara?" Alan asked as he looked around the table.

"Nothing's changed over here," Randy said. "We offer Nate a spot at the top of our South American operations and see if he wants it. Bring him into the fold slowly, see if he works out and if he's hungry for more. We already know he's smart enough. We'll call the shots, see if we're comfortable with him. Show Nate and Sara the tools in our network and set him up at the ranch in Ecuador. He's had a look at the consequences. If it works out, he might even take over one of our spots. Good talent is hard to come by."

Gene nodded his head in agreement, saying, "Meanwhile, we spin the day-to-day operations of the drug business off to Whip McCalister and the Incan, Blackie. Won't miss a beat, gentlemen. Petty cash is still healthy."

Mike O'Neal piped in, "Let's stop beating this dead horse. Are we still expecting them by twelve? Let's wrap the small potatoes up. My plane's ready to go."

Alan Calaway responded, "They will be here in about fifteen minutes. The driver picked them up at the airport an hour ago. We should be out of here by two o'clock. I'm with O'Neal. I've got a four o'clock tee time."

Calaway looked at John, then spoke to the group.

"How's the chest, John? That lightweight Kevlar vest came in mighty handy. Not the first time you've been shot and something tells me it won't be your last. Lucky for you that operation came out clean. I read the teams debriefs, yours is missing. Didn't even chance leaving DNA or fingerprints on the packages or case. Gotta love that arousal stuff. Good planning until the very end. Seriously, John, a wild west gunfight? Did you plan on stepping in for your niece and her husband all along or did you override our vote at the last minute? Nate and Sara showed some moxie though. That couple's going to fit right in."

Alan scratched his nose and asked, "What are you going to do with Gordon Manners? By now he's surely figured out there isn't a bank account.

How mad do you think he is, John. Do you think we should give him back the real Picasso?" Calaway broke out in a laugh. He liked needling John.

John didn't see any point in discussing the subject further. Calaway didn't push it.

Chapter 36

Too Good To Be True

Nate and Sara had prepared for the worst. They were afraid they had been recognized by the detectives, but Uncle John assured them they were in the clear. The meeting with the detectives was more like an interrogation, but at least it was short, concise, and stayed on point. Detective Gibbs asked the questions while Detective O'Hare listened and scratched a few notes onto a pad of paper. The interview consisted of questions such as where had they been for the last week, where were they the night of the murders, did they know the dead men, why a fake funeral; it was nothing Nate and Sara couldn't handle. It ended with routine questions covering family, jobs, and monthly bills.

To prepare, Nate had cross-examined Sara over and over, covering the facts and, more importantly, the specifics. They went over the bogus charges that showed up on their credit card statement and worked out the timeline of their "vacation." They even Googled the hotels they never stayed in to get a picture of what they looked like, just to be on the safe side. As the two rode the elevator up that morning, Nate gave Sara one last pop quiz on the rules for testifying.

"What are the three best answers you can give?"

Sara looked at the floor. "Yes, no, and I don't know."

"Right. And if you have to talk, what then?"

"One sentence," Sara replied.

Nate had done this a thousand times, preparing clients for cross-examination.

"And how long is a sentence?"

Sara took a deep breath.

"Four to six words. Never talk in the narrative and never, ever engage them in conversation. I got it, Nate. It's you I'm worried about."

The interrogation went smoothly and Detective Gibbs never asked the hard questions, or maybe the couple had simply studied too hard.

After Nate and Sara met with the detectives they continued to follow the e-instructions, only this time they had been given personally by Uncle John. The two caught a private plane to Colorado Springs.

"Expect the best, but always prepare for the worst," Sara said to Nate as they boarded the twin-engine Beechcraft King Air.

When Nate entered the plane his eyes lit up and a wide grin came across his face. "Nice!" was all he managed to say as he took in the plush cabin that was set up as a small conference room with tan leather chairs surrounding a shiny faux wooden table.

A stranger in a blue blazer and jeans swiveled his chair around at the table.

"Mr. and Mrs. Level. I have been looking forward to meeting you. My name is Wade Mayfield. I'm here to brief you before the meeting. It's a two-hour flight and I've been sent to go over the preliminaries with you. I can get most of your questions answered during our flight," the man said. He stood up and shook Nate's, then Sara's hand.

"Nice digs," Nate said.

"Thanks. Now, why don't you two buckle up and we'll get the show on the road," he said.

The airplane touched down in Colorado Springs and taxied into a private hangar. Nate and Sara left Mr. Mayfield on the plane and climbed into the backseat of an awaiting black Cadillac Escalade. *Of course it was black*, Nate thought. Their questions, for the most part, had been answered, but their decision wasn't made.

"Never look a gift horse in the mouth. You have wanted to stop your law practice for years. Let me see if I got this right…" Sara said.

She went over their briefing.

"Oversee an established multibillion-dollar conglomerate dealing in real estate, agriculture, construction, and investments, from a 915,000-acre ranch in Ecuador. Comes with a corporate jet, a base salary of half a million a year, with a quarterly bonus, and your staff is experienced waiting to meet you in offices all over South America."

"You know what they say, Sara," Nate retorted. "If it sounds too good to be true, it isn't."

The Escalade traveled at a comfortable cruising speed for less than an hour. The trip was a scenic wonderland. Open pastures framed in green pines with snow-capped mountains shooting up in the background. The sky was translucent, accented by fat white clouds floating by. They traveled over the top of a mountain and the valley below came into view. It reminded Sara of a Norman Rockwell painting, peaceful and serene. They turned off the main road and crossed an old wooden bridge. The sound was an enchanting, "Clickity clack. Clickity clack." Underneath the bridge, a crystal clear stream flowed over the shallows, bubbling white around smooth, round river rock. The Escalade turned into a gated driveway. A two-story brick estate surrounded by massive evergreens and well-manicured gardens came into view. The driver stopped and exchanged niceties. He explained that the meeting was going to be taking place in the study, first door to the left off the grand foyer. Nate could have sworn when he exited the car that he saw something move on the roof. After what he had just been through he figured it was security, armed to the teeth.

As they entered the study, a man stood and crossed the room.

"Welcome to my humble abode. Allow me to introduce you to the Commission," he said with a big smile and a pat on Nate's back.

"The name's Alan Calaway. You can call me Alan," he said as he started the introductions. "Of course, you already know your dear ol' Uncle John." He pointed to Uncle John sitting next to the fireplace.

Nate was frozen. Sara, for reasons unbeknownst to her, curtsied and muttered, "Mr. Vice President."

Calaway replied, "Not for long. I only have another year as second fiddle. Might just get out of the public life altogether." He gestured the two over to the black walnut table.

Calaway went on with the introductions, pointing out "That's Senator Mike O'Neal from the great State of Texas." Mike O'Neal did not stand but instead offered a queen-like wave.

"That's Mr. Randy Jones, currently sits on the Board of Directors for Starbucks, Kinder Morgan, and a bunch of those other companies like Union Pacific Railroad, Maersk Shipping, and the like." Randy Jones shook a guns-up signal with his right hand.

"And last but not least, we have Mr. Gene Weber. He's, well…
logistics."

Gene rose and shook both Sara and Nate's hand.

Calaway nodded in approval.

"Now that introductions are over, let's get down to business, shall we?"

Choices Make The Man

Detective O'Hare was feeling rather good about himself. To keep his aging body on track these days, he always tried to work out in the gym at least three times a week. This morning, though, his routine workout was charged with a comfort he couldn't remember feeling in a long, long time. He always started his workout by doing sit-ups, a goal of 70 that he rarely pushed himself to achieve. He would then hit the weight machines to keep his muscles toned and to loosen up. At his age he didn't need to buff up for the ladies, so when it came to lifting weights he was a tried and true believer in the low-weight, high-repetition philosophy. Don't pull a muscle trying to lift too much, lift enough to do some good, and compensate the lower weight with more lifts. Nowadays, pulled muscles were more painful than they used to be and although he wouldn't admit it to himself, they took longer to heal. A lot longer. If he had time he worked the punching bag to keep his reflexes in check and would go three rounds with the heavy bag to break a good sweat. This all loosened him up for his swim.

Once during a yearly physical, an orthopedic surgeon told him his best customers came to him by way of the cardiologist. Joggers ran for cardio and to help their heart, but after years of jogging, it destroyed their knees. O'Hare had undergone two knee surgeries on his right knee and needed a fix on the left, but not because of jogging. A result of hard physical labor when he was young coupled with youthful mismanagement catching up to him with age. One of the reasons he swam for exercise.

The workout goal after warming up was to swim a mile at a brisk pace, followed by 15 minutes in the steam room. The bar was often lowered to two swims close to 1/2 mile each, and lollygagging in the steam for as long as he could stand it. After he finished whatever workout he could muster these days, a shower always followed and then it was off to the office.

But today was different. The sit-ups came easy, so he bumped a few extra for good measure. He added more weight on the machines and finished all the reps. The swim was fast and relaxing with the turns at the edge of the pool smooth as glass. He cranked the whole mile and did two extra laps to cool down. He also stayed in the steam room for an easy 15.

He didn't know why it came so easy this morning. He was just feeling good about himself. Maybe it was the notoriety he was getting from stopping one of the most dangerous drug lords on the face of the planet, or maybe it had something to do with him closing another homicide. Whatever it was, it agreed with him. He felt the itch to roll some bones. Heading over to the Coushatta Indian Reservation this weekend with the wife seemed like a fine idea.

To reward himself on the success of his workout, he decided to stop at his favorite breakfast spot. When he walked into the donut shop, he grabbed an orange juice and stood in front of the long glass display case. They had it all. Sugar glazed, icing, plain, blueberry, cinnamon, jelly filled, fried or baked. Bacon, egg, and sausage biscuits, bagels, Kolaches, boudin, you name it. He took a step back, wondering if he should go all out. He loved this place.

"Decisions, decisions," he said out loud as he rubbed his chin.

As a bell on the front door jingled, he turned around to see a small girl about eight years old holding a raggedy stuffed dog with long floppy ears in one hand and her father's hand in the other. When the child saw the display case, she let go of her father's hand and rushed up to the case, directly in front of the blue glazed donuts covered with colored sprinkles.

"Ohhhhh, Daddy. Look, look, look!" the little girl said with a bright smile and wide eyes as she smudged her fingers on the glass in front of the sprinkled blue donuts.

Her father followed her up to the counter saying, "Pick out the one you want," and then went on to order two sausage cheese Kolaches and a dozen glazed to go.

The father looked down at his daughter, still mesmerized in front of the blue icing donuts with sprinkles.

"Is that the one you want? Are you sure?" he asked.

O'Hare could tell she wasn't sure. She needed time, after all, before making such an important decision.

The little girl hugged her stuffed dog as she played with her long blond hair, twisting it slowly around her index finger. She moved down the display case, going from one flavor to the next, stopping every few feet to put her finger on the glass in front of one treasure, then another.

"You want that one?" her father asked when her finger touched the glass in front of a yellow jelly-filled, but the girl didn't say a word and moved on down the long case.

She stopped again, pointing with her little fingers. The Dad knew this was going to take a minute, so he crouched down at eye level with his daughter.

"Is that the one you want?" he asked again, but his baby girl quickly shook her head, firmly saying "No" and moving on.

So he stood up and put his hand on top of the little girl's head, giving her long hair a light tussle.

"Which one are you going to get, Sis?" he asked as he watched his daughter reach the end of the glass display case. No more magic, the field had been surveyed, the subject studied. Now was not the time to think, it was time to act. For her, it was time to make a life-changing decision.

The baby girl glanced up at her father, her face still beaming with a wide smile, and proceeded to skip all the way back down to the other end of the display case. She put her finger on the glass in front of the blue donuts with colored sprinkles.

"That one!" she commanded. The choice was made. She knew from the moment she walked in which one she wanted. But she had to be sure. She had to take her time, look at all her options, gauge the consequences, and weigh the facts. She was now satisfied with her decision. She wrinkled her mouth and nose to the side of her face and gave a quick, confident nod of the head that tossed her uncombed blonde hair up and down. The confirmation of her final decision. The right choice, not made in haste. It was well thought out, and she beamed with a sense of accomplishment and self-fulfillment. She danced from foot to foot as the lady behind the counter handed her a white sack holding the prize. Life's choices.

O'Hare did not mind the wait. He continued to watch as the baby girl confidently clutched the dream close to her loyal dog, grabbed her father's hand, and skipped away. The bell on the door jingled as they walked out.

It was now Detective O'Hare's turn. He stepped up. "Give me one of those large bacon, egg, and cheese biscuits with jalapenos and a dozen glazed donuts. To go please."

As the waitress started to load a dozen into a box, he changed his mind.

"You better make those donuts blueberry. I work with a health nut."

J. Price Blalock is an attorney in Kemah, Texas. He has been married for thirty-eight years and has three grown children. He lives with his wife Lynn and their dog Colt on Galveston Bay. His passion is the outdoors. Fishing, birding and water sports. He dedicates this book to true friends, loyal family and fun.

www.ingramcontent.com/pod-product-compliance
Lightning Source LLC
Chambersburg PA
CBHW051506170626
46811CB00002B/677